Getting Through It

Contents

Chapter 1 - Craw 3

Chapter 2 - Starting Block 7

Chapter 3 - Legacy 13

Chapter 4 - Mortified 18

Chapter 5 - Leadership 27

Chapter 6 - Characters 36

Chapter 7 - Religion 39

Chapter 8 - Savior 44

Chapter 9 - Greater Expectations 46

Chapter 10 - A Waste 52

Chapter 11 - Harness 59

Chapter 12 - Covet 74

Chapter 13 - Purpose 79

Chapter 14 - Fly on a wall 81

Chapter 15 - Sex Appeal 82

Chapter 16 - Daily Escape 85

Chapter 17 - Civilized 88

Chapter 18 - Looking glass 93

Chapter 19 - Finicky 97

Chapter 20 - Fat Head 99

Chapter 21 - Transition 104

Chapter 22 - Depart 107

Chapter 1 - Craw

In the early morning there is a crowd of suits, wool coats and shiny black shoes that walk into the buildings downtown. The buildings lean in the morning light towards the Charles River.
Walking up to the building Mark's shoes always feel heavier. It is a slightly denser weight than a small child, but less than a Volkswagen. Despite the added pressure each morning he still finds his way to his desk and checks his emails. Inside his chest his heart usually sinks to about where his stomach is and jumbles during the last moments of digestion.
The other people around his space will set their bags down and race to the free coffee and tea in the break room.
The feeling of joy when a flavored hot beverage that you have not paid for touches your lips is almost orgasmic.
Mark's most peaceful few moments in the day are when he checks a few blogs and generally stares at his screen before the onslaught of emails start to come in. He likes to contemplate the amount of lint that is in his navel at any given time, as well as what will happen if a piece of furniture, like a desk, rotates on one of its legs. What will it hit? How will it complete its rotation? With the right amount of yaw, roll and tilt, will it be able to flip upside down?

When Mark's boss, Matilda Hew, plops down behind her desk in the morning she usually has to move her files from one side of her desk to the other. She does not actually look at or in them, instead she just reads the titles and holds the heavy manila folders in her hands as she passes them from one side to the other. The weight of the folders gives her a cocktail of feelings. The spectrum ranges from a sense of responsibility to dread that something has to be done within an urgent timeline.
Matilda religiously buys coffee on her way to work with multiple espressos added to it. The caffeine jolt is like an electric charge that brings some life to her in the morning. Her body craves the caffeine like a teenage girl craves losing her virginity after the high school prom.

When she comes in she immediately closes the door to her office so that she can peacefully set up her desk for the day. Each morning when she looks at the piles of paper in front of her, she is slightly frustrated. If she could make them go away with a snap like Mary Poppins she would, instead she reads illegible writing and battles with all levels of bureaucracy that sit above her. After staring at the papers that have to be filed or faxed or photocopied a faint whisper of rage overcomes her skin as she thinks of the people who asked her to do this work or simply just put it on her desk. If any of them were capable they would not bother her and go back and do their job. She is stuck with these stupid asinine paper-shuffling tasks and all she can do is push the papers through and try to figure out how to make things work.

When Noelle arrives in the morning she makes a point to say hello to everyone. If there is someone along her route that she does not greet her conscience weighs heavily on her, and she will make it a point to go by their desk as early as possible to say hello.

She double fists the free coffee in the morning even though it makes her a bit shaky around eleven o'clock from withdrawal. There is an air freshener underneath her desk because she has a few intestinal problems that leave her quite gassy throughout the day.

Deep down she hates working at Randley Financial Brokerage, but she likes to be around lots of people and desks. She would leave, but she doesn't know where she would find another office with people like this.

"Hey Matilda."

"Hey Noelle."

Noelle sits at her desk and enters the password for her computer. She neatly places her two cups of coffee in their cup warmers so that they retain their heat while she drinks them.

Noelle has a collection of porcelain gnomes and tiny puppies on her desk. It is a small collection and specifically does not get in the way of her paperwork. She admires her collection during the day. She feels a great amount of pride in her taste of the porcelain dolls. Most people wouldn't know that they are collectors items.

She sees a mass of paper stapled on her desk. It is the beginning of a wire transfer that her financial advisor started and left for her to finish. The brothers she works for are sweet to her and occasionally give her coffee and things to eat. When she comes in, she tries to be an example of sunshine and courtesy to them. Usually they smile back at her and appreciate her, but too much Noelle can get annoying.

"Hey Maria."

"Hey Noelle, how are ya?"

Maria is always in at eight o'clock so she can leave at four to pick up her daughter. She is a young girl who grew up in East Boston in an Italian family. The job is good for her because she needs the money to raise her daughter and the earlier hours help with being able to pick up her daughter. Her Aunt Joanne is the Compliance Officer for the office. Her Aunt Susan works in the operations department. Her mother works part time in the file room. Maria hates her job and spends most of her time looking at shoes and clothes online.

Her daughter, Vittoria, is a reminder of purpose and love and also what stops her from having freedom.

Mark comes into work with his exercise bag slumped over his shoulder like normal. Mark is medium height, medium build and has very small ears, which no one seems to notice. He drops his bag by his desk and inputs his password. Mark sits in front of Matilda's office and is the general gopher for Matilda and the branch manager. He takes care of any problem in the office that comes across the desk of his managers. Technically, he is part of management, but in reality he has no say in anything involving the management of the office. When there is a management meeting he chimes in on subjects that he feels he can contribute to, but for the most part is ignored. There is good reason for why he is not treated as part of management, he does not know very much about running the office. He does all the work assigned to him; and asks for more and if he can help in any way.
He's in charge of ordering office supplies, and when he can he tries to order a couple of extra toner cartridges or cork boards so he can sell them on EBay.
"Hey Mark."
"Hey Noelle, what's going on?"
"Not much."
Noelle doesn't really like Mark. When he first started working she would be terribly friendly, and he responded nonplussed due to the knowledge of the crappy job he had just taken. After that she found more things wrong with him. It became a game and she would tell Maria and Ly about how he annoyed her. Ly works alongside Maria and Noelle. She is the youngest person in the office next to Mark. She is straight out of college and is in a job as a glorified secretary. She feels as though her time in school was a complete waste. She has had the same boyfriend since her second day in college. She grew up in a Vietnamese household. Her parents immigrated to the U.S. in the 70's; her father was a mechanic for a while and then started a duck farm. Ly smokes tobacco and marijuana. When she is nervous she masturbates. She masturbates three times a day. She wants to be a table and placemat decorator, but is afraid people will make fun of her for it.
"Hey Noelle."
"Hey Ly."
As Ly gets settled Noelle looks over to her and whispers, "How was last night with Zack?"
"OK. He is such a lazy piece of crap sometimes though. We go out to dinner at this, like, really nice Italian restaurant and he doesn't even take his baseball cap off until like halfway through dinner. I was so mad. He acts just like a jerk sometimes.
"We still went home and had a nice night, but he just got tired after like the first

time and I couldn't really wake him up. What a loser." Ly sits in her chair and moves her cup of Starbucks coffee until she is comfortable.

Maria turns around and chimes in. "I know. When Carlo is like in the fucking mood it lasts like five minutes, and then he is out to the world; what a pig. If I even think of trying to do it myself he gets offended and pouts for a week. Fuckin' loser."

"Well William is a nice guy. We always go out and have some drinks, then go home. I like when he massages me or when we just cuddle on the couch and watch TV." Ly and Maria look at each other and agree at contempt for Noelle and go back to their work.

"Maria, can you make out what this is?" Noelle says to Maria.
"What is?"
"This note from Kevin. I think it says: with shred stone onere."
"I have no fucking clue what that means."
"He always does this. I never should have gotten him that book."
Noelle had gotten one of her brokers a puzzle book for Christmas and he had now taken cryptology up as a hobby while he was talking to his clients and trying to talk them in to buying in to a new investment strategy.
Noelle stood up from her desk with the note and walked towards Kevin's office. She was annoyed and she wanted Kevin to stop the stupid notes that she didn't understand. When she got to the doorway she saw that he had just come in his office, but his back was to her. She raised her hand to knock on the doorway, but before her hand hit the trim of the door she noticed he had his hand down his pants and was scratching his genitals.
Noelle felt embarrassed and decided to walk back to her desk and ask about the note later.

Chapter 2 - Starting Block

Richard walks in to his office and looks for any disturbed papers or signs of life. He has been in his office for fifteen years but he still has not put up any pictures. All the pictures in his office are laying on their side or leaning against a wall. Some are frames of inspirational phrases stitched in to fabric and others show a comic or cartoon associated with his position as the manager. The pictures on the ground help remind him of how temporary his job can be. Even though he has had success and held his ground with his office, he still has heard too many stories of other managers who do well by bringing in more brokers and then get stuck in a messy arbitration or give bad advice and lose a client. All of these stories remind him of how temporary his position is. On his desk is the obligatory wall street journal and some other magazines about changes or trends or statistics that have happened in the field. While thumbing through an article about the top performing hedge funds of the past year he dog ears a page that seems worthy of photocopying and puts the magazine on his desk. After setting the magazine down he notices that one of his chairs is turned slightly more to its right. He gets up and moves the chair so that it is in perfect symmetry with the other. This is a morning ritual of his. He knows that invariably by the end of the day with all the meetings and traffic of people coming through his office that it will be moved and in disorder, but he likes starting the day with order. With his magazine in his hand he sits back in his chair and starts to thumb through the days reading material. To his left on the top drawer of the desk he notices a booger he had discarded from the day before. He wonders why the cleaning staff doesn't do a better job.

Matilda enters her office before 7:10 in the morning and places her turbo hot triple espresso on her desk. She doesn't come in early because she likes her job; in fact she hates her job. She comes in early because there is a certain amount of things she must do during the day and people always seem to take up her time. She can't get much done during the day and wants to try and accomplish something while no one bothers her.
Sitting in her little office across from Richard she has a clear view that he is in and busy reading. She thinks he comes in early because he just wants to get out of his house.
Looking at her computer screen she tries to remember her password. It is one of her kid's names. Trying to remember which one is a weight on her mind. She feels almost embarrassed when she has problems trying to remember one of the names of her five children. Matilda enters the password and waits for the machine to accept it. As the machine slowly checks it databanks on the secured

intranet she contemplates if they have fired her or not. It is a silent dream she has in the morning. Even though she would not have the means to support her children, most likely lose her home, not have enough to pay her lawyers so she can still battle her ex-husband who tries to sue her monthly it still would be worth it not to come in to work.

She gulps from her Dunkin' Doughnuts jumbo cup and is let in to the system. Microsoft Outlook comes up and she sees that she has about fifty unread emails. Mostly they are annoying things that she will never read or confirmations of orders being placed or the shipment or arrival of new equipment.

Matilda scans the titles of the subjects quickly and tries to delete the unnecessary emails as quickly as possible. On her desk is a giant calendar for the whole month. This calendar is what she uses to keep herself organized and in control. The calendar takes up practically the total room of her desk. She tries to write every possible thing on there because she knows it is too big to be carried out of the office or lost within the rubble. On it are phone numbers, addresses, reminders and doodles. It is the one tool of her office that she trusts because the puzzle of numbers and letters is organized in a fashion that only she knows. With two days left in the month she does not have much more room to write, but she makes do with what she has. From one email she writes in that an intern has an appointment for a drug test on Friday.

Carefully, she puts the papers that have accumulated on her desk into neat piles. To her each pile represents another block of time in her life that will be lost.

Joanne comes into her office promptly between 7:40 and 8:00. She picks up her niece on her way to work. When she arrives to the office she always starts by watering her plants. Joanne works on the twenty-eighth floor and is the representative of management there. On the twenty-eighth floor there are less people and it is much quieter. Joanne is very aggressive, confrontational and has a condescending tone that makes almost all people talk to her feel stupid. The people on the twenty-eighth floor usually go to Matilda if they have a question. Matilda is also not the nicest person to go to, but she is less likely to yell at you or make you feel stupid for asking. Part of the reason Joanne is so gruff with the people on the twenty-eighth floor is that she wants to be able to complete her work before the end of the day. Joanne suffers from neuroses similar to an autistic savant. If her files are not updated and modules not checked she goes into a slight panic at the end of the day and goes home and maniacally pets her cats.

She is the compliance officer of the office and it is her duty to ensure that the office is kept up to date on all legalities and company policy that has changed. There are also occasional seminars and colloquiums that re-inform the employees of what is and is not legal.

Her job mainly consists of harping on people until they do what the company wants them to do. She is the second most hated person in the office. The first is William Buckman. He is the financial advisor for the ultra-high net worth clients. He is considered one of the top hundred financial advisors in the U.S. according to Barron's Magazine, The Boston Globe and Wealth Management U.S.A. He stopped taking clients with less than fifty million dollars to invest in the early nineties.

Joanne sits down and logs into her machine. She looks at her clock and stares at her monitor. The machine usually takes two minutes and around thirty seconds to completely load up so she can check her mail and maneuver in the system. Today it is two minutes and fifty seconds. She wonders if Mark can do anything in particular to speed up her machine. He has been working here for only two months and he has already shown himself to be only acceptable at his job and a bit of a smart ass. Joanne doesn't mind smart asses, she grew up in an Italian family in East Boston and sarcasm and cynicism are the only ways she knows how to communicate. Mark seems a bit annoying to her though. She would like to smack him but she know which articles in the employee handbook that would go against.

She opens her outlook folder and starts checking off emails that are unimportant or not essential to read. She smiles slightly as she deletes an email from a broker. He is not a very big producer and kind of a moron so he won't put up a fight when he calls her to know her response and she explains that she didn't get the email because the system is backed up. After eighteen years in the office she has learned that most of the brokers in the officer are able to talk with confidence and sell their stock and bonds to people on the phone but in reality they are just insecure people. They are incapable of managing their own business, which is why they latch on to a bigger hive like Randley Financial Brokerage. Here they spend all their time selling and little time thinking about anything.

Matilda looks up to her phone and sees that Joanne is calling her.
"Hey."
"Hey. Guess what? Turns out I don't have cancer. Doctor says that you can't get it by putting up with whiny brats all day."
"Why am I not surprised?" Matilda says sympathetically.
"We'll just have to find workmen's comp some other way. You could always push me down the stairs," Matilda suggests.
"Yeah, but then only you would get it. I don't trust you to share any money. Besides it would take more than a few stairs to put a dent in you."
"Thanks."
Joanne clears some pesky phlegm from her throat. "So, where do we start with

Richard today?"

"Can I get him to fire Haruo? He's been bugging me lately."

"There wouldn't be any love loss in the office. But you will have to find another producer."

"Haruo doesn't produce any money," Matilda counters.

"Well then somebody to fill the void Haruo will make."

"My puppy could fill the void. He would even be more popular than that Japanese leprechaun."

"Good idea, I'll run it by HR and see what benefits package we can come up with."

At this moment there are two stock brokers in their offices starting the day. One is dialing into an international radio broadcast of the East Indies Tea Company. The other has opened up a website of a girlfriend of his from when he was in college. The girl is a bit of a free spirit raver type of girl that works at Denny's All American Restaurant and posts 'Erotic' pictures on her website. It is the closest thing to pornography that the stock brokers can access. He secretly wonders whose job it is to block all the porn sights for the company's internet. He wonders if they search for anything in particular, fetish stuff or just mainstream typical nudity and some seductive pose. Maybe they take a moment to look at the pictures or linger for only a second and then quickly switch off because of their boss is watching.

The picture of his friend has finally loaded. She's atop a black motorcycle on the beach. She is wearing a black lace thong and covering her breasts with her right arm while looking at the camera to her right side.

She has gotten a little thinner since he last saw her. He wonders if she has turned a bit anorexic.

George Stapleton arrives in his office shortly after eight in the morning. Usually he gets in around nine but he needs some extra time to review some pieces he is showing at a gallery in a few weeks. George had the fortunate experience of going to Harvard Business School and making friends that went on to run corporations and decently sized businesses. He worked hard for his first fifteen years out of school and now for the last five he has put in a medium amount of effort so that he can pursue his hobby of Art. He is a photographer and takes pleasure in photographing elements of urban nature in a comical way. His pictures usually encapsulate the feeling of a person in a moment like a guy nonchalantly sipping a Starbucks Coffee in front of a Starbucks while watching a car crash into a Starbucks on the opposite side of an intersection.

At 8:30 in the morning Ronald Dunstmeyer arrives in the office. He makes it a strict point not to come in until 8:30. He might be late by a few minutes, but he will never be early. He's the operations manager of the office. All paper work and trading processes for the office go through him. While most processes have been computerized, for everything there is a duplicate done on paper. Especially for any trades that have completed. This is to ensure that all transactions are done properly and in order.

Every piece of paper must go by Ron's desk in order to be passed along and approved. Ron reviews a few thousand transactions a day and has to solve any discrepancies along with the normal operations of a department. Ron doesn't come into the office until it is time. If he arrives early to the building he will wait until 8:29 to enter and press the up button on the elevator.

Ron hates his job. He likes the people he works with. Ron feels a very large amount of stress everyday. His wife is expecting their first baby in five months. Ron takes pleasure each day in attempting to create one more way the office can be destroyed. If possible Ron finds some way to encourage the crumbling of the company. He does not do anything to the transactions, instead he attempts to destroy the things in the office that are integral to its maintenance and operation. He might lightly kick a computer that is connected to the internal mainframe or drop a paper clip in some unknown hole of a photocopier or possibly hide a stapler or necessary tool from the manager's desk. These are all very little tasks but in these little doses he gets a lot of pleasure. The logic that he follows is that with enough ways to begin destruction, he might successfully find a way to fully degrade or corrode the office by the time he retires.

All the other ladies in the operations department love Ron because of his good nature and cute chubby cheeks. He's from Indiana and has the exact demeanor of a nice polite farm boy from the Midwest.

The ladies in the operations department don't suspect his nefarious plans but they are worried that the demands and stress put on Ron are going to lead him to bring a rather large gun into the office one day.

Ron protects the ladies in the department by controlling their responsibilities and workload. He hates his job and they hate theirs so he doesn't want to make it worse than it has to be. When they are stressed or overloaded he cuts them off from the rest of the company and public by answering their phones and telling people they are busy and that they will have to wait. Because he does this the ladies have absolute loyalty to Ron.

As Ron gets off the elevator and goes down the hallway to the operations department he sees that part of the rug in the hallway is being replaced. He checks both ways down the hallways for anyone watching. He pulls up part of the rug and tears out a piece of the stuffing from underneath. As he goes further down the hallway he tosses the piece in the trash. Now there is a slight divot under the rug in the hallway.

"Hi diddly party people," Ron says cheerfully.
"Hey Ron," says Beth.
"Hey Ronny," says Paula.
"How was darts last night?" asks Beth.
"Good. We won and the Budweiser girls were there as well."
"Budweiser chicks, what would Kira think?"
"She paid me a buck to see if I could get a kiss from one of them."
"Any takers?"
"Not quite. I think I had one girl, but then it turned out she thought I was just looking for the bathroom. It has been a while since I sprung some lines on a chick."
"That's alright, I am sure you'll get her next time," Beth replied lovingly, but sarcastically.

Ron sits at his desk and starts to go through the alternate market orders from yesterday. After reviewing the first hundred sheets he thinks about how many trees have come through his office since he has taken his job. He concludes the number must be fairly large.

After shaking his head he continues on with reviewing the transactions.

Chapter 3 - Legacy

It was a sunny and calm day when suddenly Clark Kent was swept with an unquenchable thirst. As he sat at his desk he flailed out to all directions in an attempt to seek any sign of moisture or at least to show signs of the need for help. He was shriveling from the inside as though he had swallowed an entire Bolivian salt flat. How will he be able to stop this desiccation? Will the parched patron find some way to seek his way to rehydration?

Matilda poked her head out of her office, "Mark, look in the system for the personal computing device form. Then go around and make sure that we have everyone updated."
Clicking through the Randley Financial Brokerage intranet Mark finds the form and prints out a copy. After photocopying another fifty he starts his stroll around the office. Everyone is looking very busy and seems to be doing something that keeps their fingers or mouths in motion. Mark spots a personal computer on Dan's desk.
"Hey Dan, what's going on?"
"Hey Mark, how's it going?"
Dan has been working in the office for two months. He is still on a probationary period, and even though he outweighs Mark by about twenty years he still feels slightly nervous around him because he is part of the management. One bad word in management might get to Richard and then he would be out of a job. Mark just stares for a moment at the balding Cro-Magnon size man and wonders what this man's cranium will look like when he completely lost all his hair.
"Not bad. I'm just going around updating my files on some things. You started here a few months ago, right?"
"Yeah, was there something that I didn't fill out?"
"No, no. I'm just updating my files for personal computing devices. Those are just computers or other devices that you bring in to the office and use. The computers that we give you are property of Randley Financial Brokerage, and we can repair anything we own, but when you bring your own computer in there is a little conflict."
"Oh, am I not allowed to bring it in?" Dan asked nervously.
"Oh no way man, it's fine. It is just that we need everyone who does to sign the form. You know, your typical sign your life away form that says we can search the machine just in case you might be stealing information or anything else."
"Ah, gotcha. No problem." Dan senses that Mark is trying to be more informal to ease his nervousness. This makes Dan more nervous.

"Just tell me where to sign bud and I will have no problem doing it."
"Okie dokie. Just sign your name here and date here. Thanks."
Leaving the area Mark hears Dan quickly pick up his phone and dial a number. As Mark is walking away he wonders what the man is like at home with his wife and new son.

The Cotlin group is a dynasty in the Randley Financial Brokerage office. Patrick Cotlin is an older broker who has spent a very long time building his business. He has been in the office long enough to have the business change around him, and has been able to have a lasting business while not having to change too much with it. When he started it was Storm Haroldson, then they were bought by Hancock & Sons, then they merged with Randley Financial Brokerage who just pushed out any lasting life of Hancock or his Sons. Patrick's son James is working with him. James and Antonio are both trying to take over the business that Patrick has built up. James and Antonio are a younger generation of financial advisors that are taking over the business of the profession of a Stock Broker. It's not a business anymore of selling single stocks or bonds to a client, instead you are selling an organization that has a longitudinal record of success. You sell this with words like longitudinal and success. James and Antonio have explained to Patrick what the new business is about, and how they are going about influencing 'their' clients towards the new goal. Patrick heard what they had to say. He nodded his head in understanding. Patrick still calls up the clients and encourages them to buy a bond that he thinks will make them a decent profit.

James and Antonio are less than thrilled at Patrick's actions. James and Antonio are trying to use the products that are provided by Randley Financial Brokerage to encourage the clients to invest more with the group. Here is the sales breakdown:
1. You talk to client
2. You get them to fill out a Finances and Goal Analysis
3. You look at the results of computing the amount of their salaries, family, future retirement goals, current real estate, etc. and figure out how much they should invest in order to have the future that they want.
4. Always ask for more money than the plan supposes
5. Dump it in managed accounts that have a history of gaining interest
6. Move on to next client

The new generation of stockbroker doesn't really need to be aware of trends or patterns in the stock market. Market analysis is taken out of their hands and given to some nerds in the back room who look at graphs and read articles about new products being developed in Taiwan and interpreting their effects on consumer confidence in a product that next year will be introduced by some unknown electrical engineering firm which will then be gobbled up by a powerhouse and thus the product will be integrated into a form of technology that will be easily dispensable to every home in America and the rest of the world.

James and Antonio don't have to think about products or where the market is headed in five years. They just have to get more people to give them their money so they can put it in accounts that other people manage and they can collect commission on all sales.

Mark walks down the hall toward the corner of the office occupied by the Cotlin group. With two days left in the week the group is waiting enthusiastically for the weekend. Antonio is thirty and Ron is twenty-nine.

Antonio has been married for ten years to his childhood sweetheart and has four kids, with one more on the way. His life consists of working and taking care of his kids. He coaches little league, drives to ballet, and still comes to work with a moderate amount of energy. The diplomatic skills he's learned while raising his kids has helped to keep Patrick and James from stabbing each other with their words.

James' life currently consists of planning his upcoming wedding with his fiancé. He's the type of guy who does not enjoy picking out the color of a cake or the type of flowers or the setting for his relatives. He truly does not care, but realizes that he is getting older and he found a beautiful woman to marry him so he will stomach stupid little things so that he can have a life with her.

"Mark, what's going on? Hey, I tell you what, why don't you do me a favor and order up a flat screen for me. Richard said to go ahead and put it on the company tab. Just go ahead and order it, it is in the works." Antonio says with much gusto.

"You know, that sounds like a great idea and as soon as Richard tells me he wants to order you a flat screen, I will do it."

"Richard told me, come on, don't worry about it."

"Oh, I'm not. These flat screens, why do you want one anyways? I mean, they hurt your eyes less than the regular monitors, they are more compact so they allow you more room for your desk, they even match the color of the desk a little better. Why on earth would you want one anyways?"

Antonio looks at Mark with one eyebrow cocked and gives him a smile.

"So, the reason that I have graced you with my presence today is that I need to make sure that I have the proper forms signed for anyone who has a separate computer here in the office. Just like that palm pilot on your desk there Antonio. If you have a computer here in the office you need to sign a form that says that we can essentially check it any time we want in the event we think you are stealing secrets, blah blah blah. Do me a favor and sign and date here and I will be on my way."

"Wait, so if I bring this in here you want me to sign a piece of paper that says that you will be able to search through it if you want to?"
"Precisely."
"No way. Why would I do that?"
"Well that palm pilot has the ability to store information. If you want to you could transfer data on to it from the computer. So if you want to be able to bring that machine in the office you will have to sign the form."
"Fine then, I won't bring it into the office anymore." He said resolutely while putting the Palm Pilot into the desk drawer.
"So you are not going to bring that into the office ever again?"
"No." Antonio said with his best smile.
"Fine, I will remember that."
Patrick came out of his office with his umbrella in his hand.
"How's it goin' Marcus?"
Patrick always calls Mark Marcus. Mark doesn't particularly know why except that in the office the giving of nicknames is a very popular pastime. Not too many things rhyme with Mark. Bark, hark, lark, narc? Mark has concluded that Marcus is Patrick's final conclusion for a pet name after an exhausting creative brainstorm.
Without waiting for an answer Patrick turns to Ron and Antonio and says, "I am headed out for a few hours. I am going to see Walt Peterson for lunch and see if he wants to come in for a meeting next week."
"Right-o chief." Antonio says with a wry smile.
After Patrick has left ear shot Ron says, "Ten bucks says he sells ten bonds to Peterson before the end of tomorrow."
"I won't take that bet," Antonio says taciturnly. "But give us a meeting with the guy and we will bring him into the Cotlin group and put the rest of the money where it should be."
"Yeah, but that means we will bring him in with ten thousand less dollars than we could have before. Fuck, I wish he would listen to us once in a while and just do like we have planned."
William Dorey has his desk aligned with Antonio and Ron. He is there to view all their bickering and conversations and usually chooses not to be part of them. He is giving his business over to the group because he has realized that he is getting on in years and does not want to sit at his desk forever. He figures he has a few more years taking phone calls and being part of the team meetings and then he can quietly move out of the office and into a life of playing golf a few times a week.
"To be honest I don't know why you guys are bickering about a few bonds. These clients have been doing business with your dad for years and if he tells them about something that he thinks would be a good idea, they will listen

because they trust him. The product that you are selling is good and reliable, but when these families have no experience with anything on the market. They need to trust your opinion and when you sell something to them that is new and different the clients are going to be hesitant. So, let your father sell them a few bonds because it is what they are used to and when the time comes your father will tell them that your plan is what they need to do."

When William gives advice or criticism James and Antonio listen. William does not do it very often and when he does it is usually concise and to the point. William does not bully or lecture James and Antonio about the business that he has been in for forty years, instead he knows that James and Antonio will figure out what their business will be and how to make it work.

James and Antonio spend all their hours during the day talking to people and figuring out a plan for how they are going to approach certain clients.

They figure that there are two different ways that they will make it in the business. One is through many years of taking in clients and converting them into this business model that has been put before them. The other is to suddenly get dropped a large amount of ultra-high net worth clients which they will cow tow to their every need while getting paid vast sums of money for putting in orders.

They hope for the latter.

Chapter 4 - Mortified

It's 10:00 in the morning and Haruo is sitting behind his desk looking at the wall. The wall itself is painted a shade of white and after a year has collected dust and other forms of dirt. He looks at the wall daily. He finds it more soothing than putting up a picture of a sailboat like other people in the office. He has not had a client call him all day. When he calls clients he only gets the recording machine. He tries to leave a safe and succinct message, but is always nervous that they are actually screening his message and are actually listening while he is talking. He believes that if he is talking to them directly through the machine he should have a friendly and open voice. Although, if they are not actually screening their machine and instead will listen to his message at a later time, it just sounds like an over friendly and creepy message from the guy that is buying and advising your investments. Haruo is paranoid of this. Haruo thinks his clients hate him because he is half-Japanese. He would sue them, but he is trying to make them money. He is very conflicted.

Haruo received an email from one of his clients today. It could more appropriately be called a piece of hate mail. The client was referred to him from one of his other clients two years ago. In two years Haruo's recommendations have not made the client any money. In fact the client has lost ten thousand dollars of his original five hundred thousand. The letter informed Haruo that his services were not needed any more and that he could, "Take a long walk off of a short pier and fall on a piling on the way down."

This correspondence has put Haruo into a bit of distress. He is going to lose a client with a sizeable amount of money and is also afraid that a copy of the email has been blind carbon copied to one or all of the managers. This bothers him because he thinks the managers are all talking about him behind his back and saying racist remarks about him and thinking of ways to get him fired.

He looks pensively at his desk, deciding what the next move is in this chess game with the office managers. Should he probe them and figure if they are plotting against him or should he find something else to do. The thought of outsmarting the managers and doing some reconnaissance is too tempting. He decides he needs to take a quick confidence breather first. He fishes down to the bottom of his desk where he hides a piece of aluminum foil with a small amount of white powder.

After quick jaunt into the bathroom he puts his suit jacket on and walks downstairs to the twenty seventh floor where he will begin his survey of the managers.

He walks slowly out of the stairwell into the hallway and starts with a little swagger. He blindly smiles and points a finger hello to no one in particular as he walks down the hall towards Matilda's office. With a sly smile he walks up towards her office and sees Mark sitting at his desk. Mark's desk is about ten feet in front of Matilda's office. He sees Mark looking at him and sidles up to his desk and puts his hand on the monitor.

Mark saw him walking down the hallway in his normal made up swagger that seemed like it was invented out of some crappy hustler movie. He saw Haruo throw a smile and finger to no one and mentally slapped him. Mark now sees Haruo is headed for his desk and is hoping he can go through the ordeal without letting on too much that he does not like Haruo.

"Hey Mark, how are you today?" Haruo says with fake charm.
"Hey Haruo" Mark says while mentally thinking, "Haruo just fucking leave."
"Is Matilda in her office right now or wandering about?"
"She is in there, but really weighed down with paperwork. Is there something I can help you with?"
"Um, hmmmmm, sure maybe. I was wondering did you get that email today about the internal audit we should be receiving soon?"
"Yeah I did. It is possible that we won't get audited though. There are only two weeks left in the auditing calendar and there are still many branches that need to be audited. It is possible that we will not be hit up."
"But you did get the email?" Haruo asked directly. Haruo feels that the eyes are windows into the soul. If Matilda or Richard got the email he feels that Mark would have heard about it and therefore would be just as reliable a source.
"Yeah. I got the email," Mark answered. Mark thinks Haruo is an idiotic failure and would like to say anything to get him away from his desk.
Haruo thinks he sees no lie in Mark's eyes and breathes a sigh of relief inside.
"Ok, no problem. I was just curious if the management was in the know as well or if it was just us on the floor. Thanks so much Marcus." Mark dislikes it when Haruo calls him Marcus.
Haruo leaves Mark's desk and goes back to the stairwell feeling that he has escaped any reprimand from the management about the client he has lost.
As Haruo leaves Mark mutters under his breath, "Fucking Haruo. Probably lost another client."

Walking back to his office Haruo feels like there is no weight on his shoulders. His feet feel lighter and he notices he is about to enter his office because he is walking so quickly. He does not want to go back inside just yet; he will visit his office neighbors and ask see what progress they are making. Haruo sees Leo in his office with a storyboard on the wall behind him. Leo is matching pieces of construction paper cut outs with folders pasted on the storyboard.

"Hey Leo, how's it going?"

Leo looks up with beady nervous eyes. "Haruo, what's going on?"

"Not much, I am just making out how I am going to land a two million dollar guy."

"Oh, hey, wow. Two million? Man who is that?"

"He is brother of one of my clients. It will be easy. I am just waiting for the right time." Haruo adjusts his pants and walks up to the story board. "What is this you have going on here?"

"I am just organizing my potential candidates for the upcoming retirement convention with the universities in the area. I think I can get most of the professors to throw me their 403b's and then I will start working on the rest of their assets."

"Looks like you are bound to corner the geriatric market." Haruo says with slight condescension.

Leo didn't pick up on the little taunt. "I'm definitely narrowing my clients to those who are in the later part of their life. I think I can make my business out of starting with these retirees and then going down the family line. I got the idea from the trickle-down effect from the Reagan era." Leo has been a Republican supporter since he was five years old when his Grandfather told him that if he wants to buy candy he needs to make his own money, and only Republicans are here to make money.

"Well, I see a definite way to make money doing that. I prefer to hunt after the big ones and reel them in, but this seems like a good idea."

"So far so good. We'll see."

Haruo walked out of Leo's office and towards the desk of his assistant. There are two assistants for six brokers on the twenty-eighth floor. All of the brokers do not make enough money in order to have their own assistant, so they must share.

Haruo moseyed over to the desk of Justin, and put a palm on his desk. Justin looked up from his cell phone that he had been texting his girlfriend.

"Justin, how's it going?"

"Not bad Haruo. What's going on?"

"Did you send out those wires that I put on your desk this morning?"

Justin looked at his barren desk and then up at Haruo.

"There were not any wires on my desk this morning."

"Yes there were. I put them there the first thing when I came into the office."

"Haruo, there were no wires here when I came in. Are you sure that they are not on your desk right now?"

"Yes, I'm sure."

"OK, I will check just to make sure."

Justin stands up and walks out from around his desk into Haruo's office. He

finds the wires on top of Haruo's desk.
"Oh, there they are. Can you get those wires taken care of?"
"Haruo you are fucking incompetent asshole and I would push you out the window if it was open. Why do I have to work for an idiot like you? I just want a fucking chance to get on a team that actually makes money and does something other than your shitty little no money wires and fucking paperwork," Justin thinks at that moment.
"No problem Haruo."
Justin goes back to his desk and looks at the paperwork. He notices that only five of the ten pages are filled out. Of the five pages the signatures and information are done in pencil. Justin heads into Haruo's office.
"Haruo, all the information is not here. Also, the signatures are not in ink. I can't wire this."
"Let me see that." Haruo looks at the first couple of pages. "Just go over it in ink and fill in the information for the last pages."
"Haruo, I can't do that, it must be done by the client. There is information missing on the payout and they need to elect what they want for which account it is going into."
"Just fax it over to them and have them fill it out. They should be in right now."
"Haruo, I have told you that all wires must be originals for me to process them. You need to send these back to them and have them fill out the information."
Justin wants to put a stapler through Haruo's head.
"I need to have those wires in today," Haruo stares at Justin matter-of-factly.
"Here, give them to me, I will do what I can."
Justin hands him the papers and walks back to his desk.
"Fucking Haruo," Justin says with clenched teeth.

Every other Thursday the younger crowd in the office goes to a local bar and drinks for a few hours. The beer is always cheaper on Thursday and it gives them a chance to vent together. After spending eight hours a day together they find that they have nothing in common except for their dislike for the office. The office has a mixture of cliques. Pearl and Tami live together and have a co-dependent relationship based on a myriad of inside jokes and a mutual revulsion of the office. They usually lead the office crew into the local tavern. The two girls have a natural ebullience that it is hard to say no to.
"Sweet, who gets the first pitchers?"
"Go ahead and get the first two Tami, I will buy after."
"Alright, cool. Who is not coming tonight?"
"I think Erin can't make it. She said something about her cousin's play or something. I am not sure."
"I swear if she ducks out of one more thirsty Thursday I am going to kick her

out of the club."

"And what club is that?"

"The "us going drinking after work" club. Hey, there's Kyle and Tom and Mark."

Kyle Sullivan is tall, medium built, and of Irish and German descent. His red hair and bleached freckled cheeks give him the look of a grown up cherub. He is dedicated to a baseball blog that he runs. He played baseball through college, but thought that he didn't have the talent to attempt for the professional leagues. Tom Stevenson is a shining example of what every girl dreams about. He is a tall muscular brunette man from Indiana. He speaks rarely and when he does it he is quiet. He has always been the best athlete on any team that he has been on. In high school he won state wide recognition his senior year for winning the big football game against the school rival. He caught the last throw with .4 seconds left in the game.

Due to Tom's shyness about his past success, no one in the office knows of his legendary status. Instead he is just a handsome man who has started a career in the management of the company.

Pearl is the first one to pipe up. "Hey guys, what's going on?"

"Not much, just glad there is one more day left in the week," Patrick says with a grin.

"I will go and get another pitcher," Tom says after putting his coat down.

"I will join you," Mark says.

Mark and Tom go to the bar and order a pitcher each. Mark also orders a pint of Guinness and Tom orders a pint of Bass. Each agreed previously during many thirsty Thursdays that the cheap pitchers of light beer did not qualify as something very good to drink. They both understood that starting off with a quality beer would help the segue into the flavored water of Bud Lite.

After a while most of the young crowd from the office has come into the bar and claimed a corner for themselves. The bar is loud and there are many conversations going on over the tables.

"Richard is a fucking sore loser. I swear I hate him and the way he treats all of us. He doesn't respect anyone in the office, and definitely none of the brokers' assistants," Pearl said pointing her glass to the ceiling.

Everyone around the table laughed or nodded in agreement except Mark and Tom.

"I mean, you guys know, right. Mark tell me about how Richard treats you and the crap job you have. It is alright, we all know it is a sucky job." Mark looked at Pearl with a bit of surprise.

"I don't think he is a bad guy. You are right, he doesn't give the brokers' assistants very much recognition, but that is just how he runs the office. He sees that it is Joanne's job to deal with the assistants."

"Joanne. God, that fucking bitch. I swear I hate her even more. She is such a fucking cold witch," Pearl said with bitter distaste.

Mark sensed that it was time to change the subject. After a few thirsty Thursdays he learned that the only subject talked about as much as how much they all hated the office was who was sleeping with whom.

"Yeah, Joanne can be a little tough sometimes, but what was that you were telling me about Sally Vail and that broker?" Mark said hoping Pearl would take the bait.

"Oh yeah. I forgot to tell you about that one," Pearl said with delight. "So, I heard from the assistant who sat next to this young new broker Ryan that he always left with Sally, and that one Friday night this assistant saw them at the bar in the Ritz down the street. I wonder what they did afterwards, huh?

'Yeah, so anyways, in the middle of the next week she sees Sally walking over to his desk and saying hello to him like every day. Sally calls him around lunch time every day and asks him if he wants to go out and get something to eat. In the morning there are letters in envelopes on his desk that have only his name on them, so they didn't get there by mail. Also, the assistant said that Ryan would talk about how he always said he had to work late and would try and duck out at the earliest possible time so that he did not have to leave with Sally." Pearl took a breath and gulped part of her beer.

"The assistant told me that about a week later it all stopped. And that Ryan stopped even walking over to her side of the office, and that Sally started to come in later and later and would almost run to her office as soon as she would get in. Rumor has it that Phil came back to the office after getting dinner so he could make a phone call to a client and he walked by her office and saw them doing it on the floor.

Oh man, I can't imagine seeing the two of them sweating and humping on the floor of the office. After that night, Ryan decided to break it off and Sally didn't want to. She tried to tell him that they could keep it a secret, and Ryan said that it was just fucking and that he didn't want to do anything anymore.

You can guess what happened after that. Sally cried, pleaded and begged, Ryan threw her off and went home.

Since that, I think she has focused all her attention on her yoga or shakra or something new wave spiritual like that. I don't know. She is so weird and fake hippie that I can't keep track with all her things.

But I should warn you guys," Pearl said taking another gulp of her beer and wagging a finger between Mark and Tom, "She likes younger handsome guys and she might try something on you. She likes them young and full of energy."

Pearl giggled to her self and threw an arm around Tami who was by her side talking to someone at the other end. Pearl had a way of talking that drained all energy from you. Her future husband will probably be someone that just feels to weak to run away.

"That's always good to know," Mark said sarcastically. He looked at his cup and saw that it was close to empty. He looked over at Tom's and saw that his was as well.

Mark started to stand up and felt a little off balance. The benefit of not drinking often is that it becomes more cost effective to get buzzed.

"Hey, Tom. Want me to get you another pint of Bass? I am going to get another Guinness."

"Yeah, sure." Tom went to his pocket to fish out some money.

"No, don't worry about it. You get the next one."

"Cool."

Mark walked over to the bar and ordered a pint of Guinness and Bass. He looked back at the group of his co-workers. He felt amazed at that moment that they all actually worked together at Randley Financial Brokerage. All of them looked so young. During the day everyone had a face of boredom or silent repugnance for the place they worked. Now that they were all in a bar talking and listening to music everyone was different. They actually looked happy.

He looked over the girls of the office. Some of them were cute and some were just normal. He liked the cynicism and scathing humor of the east Boston girls. The toughness in their sense of humor made them seem defiant and witty. That strength made them look a little sexier than the softer type of girls Mark was used to on the West Coast.

Looking over the girls from the bar he tried to think of which one he would like to sleep with. He knew he wouldn't do that. He'd seen enough people regret fucking a coworker to convince himself to go through with it.

Looking at the girls, he sized them up by the beauty in their faces, the size of their breasts, the look of their legs, and any number of things that could occupy his mind at the time. Out of them all, the most cute was Beth from Operations. Next was Maria Delgado and then maybe Pearl. At least when Pearl wasn't talking.

He thought for a second which of the girls he could actually stand to talk to and carry a conversation with. Surly and sarcastic Beth was at the top of the list.

It looked to Mark as though Beth was the choice if he in fact were going to sleep with somebody from the office. So what if she is six years older, he thought to himself. He made a slight nod to himself, and paid for the beers and took them to the table.

Mark put the beers down on the table in between himself and Tom and took his seat. The conversation was still on the subject of rumors of who had slept with whom in the office. The new victim was now Christopher Treeport.

Tami piped up with her story, "Treeport is such a macho horn ball. I swear he goes around the office flexing his muscles and staring at the tits and ass of every girl in the office just so that can get a hard on or something. I know of two assistants that he has slept with. I bet he also cheats on his wife when he is on those business trips that he goes on so much." Tami rolled her eyes in disgust and continues. "Have you seen a picture of his wife by the way. She is so fucking gorgeous. She was like a miss Rhode Island or something and he still has the nerve to cheat on her. Somebody should catch him and tell his wife. I swear that it is just not right for someone to do that."

"I am sure his wife will find out sooner or later. He is a piece of crap, but whatever, it is all just a phony scam with him. He goes to the gym and tries to get those muscles because he is really just a short disgusting piece of shit, and he deserves to get the crap kicked out of him," Beth said resolutely.

"Please let's get off the subject. It is just so stupid and depressing. Hey, Pearl, tell me about that guy you went out with last week," said Tami.

"Oh, well, he was nice and all. He was actually really cute and sweet. He picked me up and gave me flowers. Then we went to a restaurant in the North End and then went up to Lowell to see his sister's high school play. It was really sweet and cute, but I don't think that anything will happen. He is really nice, but I just don't think he is my type." Pearl took a drink from her glass of Bud light.

"Let's see. He is nice, cute, sweet and wants to take you to places that are fancy and nice. If this isn't your type of guy, then tell me what type you want," Beth said is a sarcastic tone.

Pearl smiled coyly and just took another sip from her glass.

Mark looked over at Beth and felt the effects of the beer inside him. He felt warm and confident, and thought it was a good time to ask a question.

"Tell me Beth, what is your type of guy?"

After Mark said this most of the people around him grew very quiet to hear the response of Beth. Mark immediately felt like everyone was looking at him. The blood was rushing to his face faster than water could come out of a firehose. In a moment everyone around him would find out if a romance was about to begin or would be crushed under the heaviest awkward weight possible.

"Oh I don't know, some guy tall, dark and handsome. Probably about thirty and likes to drink beer," Beth said with a fair amount of control. After the words left her mouth she took a sip from her glass and turned her head to another conversation at the table.

Everyone at the table was looking at Mark either directly or from the corner of their eye. Mark knew that the moment had passed and that it could not be taken back. Already partially buzzed, Mark started drinking more to mask the knowledge of his verbal slip up. It didn't take his mind off of the actual thing he said, and instead it just seemed to numb the feeling of embarrassment inside. Mark couldn't wait to leave then and there, but if he stayed and was the last one to leave he knew it would somehow save face. He was unsure why, but it seemed natural.

He decided to make his butt into a piece of lead and not move until he was the last one drinking.

After a few minutes he started tandyalking with Pearl about a few of the assistants that he didn't know about and left his memories into oblivion.

Chapter 5 - Leadership

8:28 a.m. Monday morning

All of the brokers in the office have ended their calls or closed their newspapers and started to make their way to the Green Room where the Monday morning meeting will begin. The hallway is a claustrophobic throng of suits. Mark makes his way through the (gathering of pressed single weave wool) suits saying the obligatory morning utterances:
Excuse me
Pardon me
Good morning
Hey, how was the weekend?

While Richard is near the front of the door to the Green Room he chats idly with anyone coming in about the goings on of the past weekend. A few of the brokers mill around him chatting about what went on. Richard notices everyone coming through the door and makes a mental note of who looks back at him and who shies his face away.
There is a brilliant mixture of territoriality among the Green Room. All of the brokers in the office are more or less alone in their business, but there still are contracts, treaties and truces between them. Piranhas hunt in a pack, but they are not necessarily working together.
Some of the brokers sit near each other because they have an office close to one another, some sit together because outside of the office they have a semi-social life and some sit as close to the door as they can so they can bolt as soon as the meeting is over.
The chairs are almost filled up as Mark finishes setting up the power point presentation. Richard is unleashing a top ten goal sheet today. All the brokers will know the top ten things that they must do to be able to be successful in the next two to five years.
Mark leaves the computer after telling Andy, the assistant manager, how to advance the slides and goes to the corner where the managers sit during the morning meeting. Mark takes out his pen and paper, and scribbles a haiku.

```
              With a mouse I work
          Simple, grey office machines.
               Who fucking cares?
```

It is time for the meeting. Richard stands at the front of the room in front of the projector screen which has the phrase on it, "Ten things you need to do in order to be in business in 2010."

"Hello everybody. Glad you're all here after this beautiful weekend. Last week I was in New York and was at a managers convention which went over the future of the business and also popped in to another meeting where they explained effective ways of giving a presentation. Apparently, I need to stand to the right of the screen or presentation or what have you in order to present it effectively." Richard walks slowly to the right of screen and waves his hand over the screen as though he were a hostess on a game show.

"Now all of you should be mesmerized by my powers of persuasion and ability to present an idea." Canned laughter fills the room. The brokers always laugh at Richard's jokes.

"There were some good ideas that came from the convention especially about how we all should be forming your future business and looking at where the business is going. The highlight though was seeing Donner and the Swiss heads talking about the future of the company and where we are going. These guys gave a presentation of the company that made it clear they know where we are and where we want to go. They explained their push with advertising in the US and that within two years they expect to see a bigger growth in the company as a whole. Our research department is second to none, and we especially are leading with international research as well. So far, Randley Financial Brokerage is the world leader in wealth management in every country, except the US. They know that if we can corner the US household market that that we will be able to lay siege to the rest of the world without a problem.

"They made it real clear that they are basically trying to take over the world." More canned laughter from the brokers.

"Now this business is changing from a point of view where the broker does the leg work and suggests to his clients what to buy to a more organized way of selling. We have funds and plans that are top notch and our clients should be buying into them. The Cotlin team here is an example of using one of the best tools that the company has, the FGA. How many of you know what a Finances and Goal Analysis is? How many of you have done one? This is a great tool that even I am just starting to use and learn about. You put in your clients information and then out comes all of the expected goals for their financial future.

Everyone should be using this tool and know how to use it. This is something that we all need to be pushing to the clients because it is how this business is changing. We are doing less of the selling of individual bonds and now we are selling funds and EFTs and private plans. Here is what you need to do. Make a list of all your clients and look at how they fit this criteria." Richard signaled to Andy and the projector screen came alive with the ten things you need to do to have a business in 2010.

On the screen were ten simple ways to review and change your clients. Mark looked up at the screen uninterestedly. This advice was not for him.

He felt very bored and tired on the Monday morning. Looking at the screen he wondered about the different types of ways the brokers manipulate people. Things like writing down every tidbit of information about the client, so in the future they knew about birthdays, anniversaries and when a child was going to graduate to another grade. He had also overheard some brokers contemplating how to encourage certain clients to divorce so that they could take up control of a bigger share of the revenue of the victor in the separation.

"I wonder if I should send a letter to Mrs. Harrington letting her know that Mr. Harrington was at the Lock and Smith last weekend with some college girl with one hand on her tit and the other in her pants." One broker said wily.

"Hah. I bet she wouldn't be surprised. But then you lose a million, cause' after the lawyer fees there won't be much left. Plus if he finds out it was you, then you won't get anything."

"You're right, he will take his money out of this account to pay for the divorce, but in the end I will get it all."

"Yeah right, come on. The guys rich, but not an idiot. With that bimbo wife he must had her sign a pre-nup."

"Ah ah ah," the broker said waving his finger. "As their main financial broker I have a copy of their trust birth certificates and marriage certificates and all other documents. There is no pre-nup. Otherwise I would have a copy. Mrs. Harrington loves me, and after I tell her about her husband, she will look for solace. Our sons are on the same soccer team, so I can meet her every weekend." The broker gave a little wink after he said this.

"Holy shit," the broker said with a smile. "But why would she stay with you, wouldn't she just go elsewhere?"

"Well, I know she is a lonely woman. Maybe I can help her when she is feeling vulnerable." The broker shrugs his shoulders.

"Shit, what an asshole. Good plan though."

Mark was brought back to the morning meeting when Richard said in his stern gruff voice, "And that brings me to the next one. You need to get educated. There are a dozen tests that we all need to take to see what else there is. Who doesn't have insurance? What about their CFP? The company pays for this education. What about commodities? What about taking one day a week and becoming a qualified family planner?"

Looking around the room Mark looked at the men with slight pot belly's all dressed in their suits that were more or less the same color. The suits were all a shade of dark blue or a type of grey wool. The dress shirts that they wore were all white button down. The ties were the only difference in anything they wore.

The ties were the signs of individuality. Some wore a professional type, solid color with tie tack or maybe a stripe but still bold. Some tried to show a playful personality yet still be professional by wearing a tie that had very small figures like trains or old bi-planes but in a design so that far away they looked like stripes or some design that could pass them as professional. A few of the brokers had on as a joke a tie that was a fluorescent pink or orange. These brokers were trying to be different and get a laugh out of anyone that they pass. Who would want to wear a fluorescent pink tie?
Mark felt very sad.

Richard was in the middle of explaining his eighth point about how there is a need for segmenting your book so that you drop your problem clients and clients that don't make any money when a loud crack above his head gave way to the ceiling dry wall falling. With the dry wall were a pairs of black socks and with it a body enshrouded in black. A man is falling through the ceiling and his feet hit Richard's head very hard. The initial thud against Richard's head seemed to break the surprise of someone coming through the ceiling. Richard toppled over to his right and the body that had fallen through the ceiling came to life mid-air, righting itself and landing on its feet. Almost simultaneously while the body landed softly it unsheathed a large curved sword from behind itself. The entire room was stunned in amazement. This man is a ninja.
Why is a ninja at the Monday morning meeting?
A row of brokers sitting next to the windows were sprayed with shattered glass as two more ninjas came through the windows feet first. They were wearing rock climbing harnesses that had allowed them obviously to repel down the side of the building, and then come through the window. After landing inside the room they cut the ropes that had allowed them access and leaped over the board room table that took up the middle of the room. They were now standing in a trio with the first ninja.
The first, and presumably, head ninja muttered something in an angry foreign tongue and went towards the nearest broker. With one double handed slash through the air the broker's head was flying and landed on the table. The blades of the ninja started to sing through the room. They kept control of the brokers by forcing them all into a corner away from the exit, but still executing them swiftly and efficiently.
Mark saw the entrance of the dark soldiers with amazement and did not move from his seat. Once they were ten feet from him he awoke from his stunned trance and let out a sonorous war cry.
"YYYYYYYYYYYYYYYAAAAAAAAAAAAAAAAAAAAAAAAAAAA
AAAAAAAAAAAAHHHHHHHHHHHHHHHHHHHHHHHHHHHHH
HHHHHHHHHHHHHHHHHHHHHHH!"

The ninjas did not move while he had started his yell, and after he was done advanced on him with the same speed that they had before.

Mark picked up his chair and held it in his left hand, while holding a ballpoint pen in his right, with the point out, towards the ninjas. The leader slashed at the legs of the chair and quickly the chair had two legs where before it had had four. With a deft quickness Mark threw the chair and pen at the ninja and picked up the two legs that had been cut from it. The blade had partially cut the legs off the chair, but made them into very deadly sharp pointed spears. Mark threw them at the other two ninjas, and with the confusion of the chair being thrown at their leader they did not see his incoming missiles. The freshly sharpened pegs found their way into the abdomen of the one on Mark's left, and into the throat of the one on his right. Torturous death awaited these ninja. Now he had to deal with the only the head of this deadly team of vipers.

The remaining ninja looked momentarily at his dying comrades and then raised his katana high and charged Mark with a deafening cry. Mark saw the slash start and before the ninja could cut him open and he dodged furtively and hit the floor. Mark looked up at his attacker and his next move would have to be the death of the ninja or Mark himself would soon be dead.

"Mark, why are you doing that with your eyebrows?" Matilda asked quietly next to him.

Mark was brought back to the morning meeting and was aware that ninja's had not corralled the room of brokers and instead he was sitting mildly next to the other managers.

With a slight nauseous feeling in his stomach he relaxed his eyebrows and turned his head over to Matilda.

He whispered, "I was just thinking about what tests I will need to take and what I will need to do."

"Oh, yeah. Richard wants us all to have our series seven and it is hard to make these guys take any tests for the company."

Mark nodded and looked back in the direction of Richard. He thought about the series seven and the other qualifications that were open to him. The tests were easy enough, but it required actually studying. Mark looked into his hands and wondered if he should take the tests. He thought about the office, the people, the work. It all seemed to be a blur of the future. He would have a desk, he would look at papers, approve, analyze, listen to problems and figure out the solutions. He would be here on the twenty-seventh floor or maybe the twenty-eighth where it was a little bit quieter. Some days he would work late, and after five be able to play some music while he caught up on his paper work.

Mark looked up from his hands to the door and tasted acrid bile in his mouth. He also had to go to the bathroom very badly at that moment.

The meeting was over and everyone stood up in unison and started for the door. At first there was a slight rush, but then the crowd slowed itself and swayed in slow movement while all waited until it was their turn to go through the mahogany stained door. Richard made sure to stand by the door so that he could greet anyone who he did not see earlier, and also be there in the event anyone wanted to talk to him or schedule a meeting.

Richard always looked at the brokers with a grin. Behind his grin he tried his best to respect everyone there, but after everyone was gone and he was alone in the green room he felt that they all were valuable idiots. The few in the office that he truly respected were brokers that didn't need him at all. Those few were men that had spent years finding and picking and choosing their clients. They were men who would were destined to be successful, and even though Richard was their manager he thought of them as equals. Richard felt hope for those brokers at the morning meetings. They tried, they worked, they spent time trying to build a book and reputation but truly they were all idiots. They didn't know what it took to be successful, what you had to do, where your mind had to be. They were all on a path of mediocrity. He hated mediocrity. If you are going to do something, then be successful at it. If you are going to go after a client, and you want all his money make sure you know your client and you have a plan. It is a battle. It is always a fight. When he was in the Navy he learned that there are always opportunities, and if you were ready you could take advantage. The harder you work the more opportunities there were. Richard started towards the door feeling a little fear about his men. He needs them all to work, and work hard.

If they don't, he is going to be out of a job.

Matilda looked up from her manila folder and saw if Mark was at his desk. She saw the back of his head and shouted out, "Mark there is a meeting at ten."
"Cool, I got about fifteen minutes so I will go and take care of something real quick."
"Alright. I will get the phones." Matilda thought to herself about how Mark always is walking about the office. Whenever she needs him he seems to be at a desk doing something with a computer or talking to someone. She would reprimand him more about it, except she knows that she does the same thing with Joanne. She yells at Mark sometimes, but she isn't serious about it. She thinks he knows this, but sometimes his face seems sad and scared.
It isn't all bad if your workers have some fear of you.
Matilda wished her ex-husband had some fear of her. That asshole was suing her again. She had just got her yearly bonus, and afterwards the dickhead sent her a subpoena of her financial records. He felt that the bonus offset her yearly

salary and thus he should pay less child support and alimony since her financial gain would allow her to provide a larger contribution to the family income.
She couldn't believe that the asshole is trying to pay less money. They are his kids. How can he be so heartless and cruel to take money from his kids. How can he just up and leave her after seventeen years of marriage and cheat on her with some tramp bitch in his office.
She felt tired. Sitting in her chair waiting for nothing in particular; she felt like her bones were tired. She opened up her desk and saw a Hershey's kiss lying next to the paper clips. She picked it up, felt the round edges for a second and unwrapped it and ate it. Chocolate made her feel better. It could also be that it was just the idea that something could make her feel better.

Ron Dunstmeyer got the group email Matilda had sent to the managers and was already headed for Richard's office for the weekly meeting. He stopped by the break room to get a coffee. After he put the cup under the machine he looked over to the photocopy room, and saw no one was in there. He walked over to the machine and opened up the front panel. He could see the innards of the machine. It all seemed very neat and orderly but dark. It felt to him as though it was some type of archaic device meant to torture mice or maybe distill oil from some vegetable like an onion.
He picked up two paper clips from the table that was adjacent to the machine and tossed them into the intestines of the photocopier. He closed the panel quietly and went to his waiting coffee and added some cream and sugar.

Richard sat behind his desk looking at the stacks of paper piled there. He touched a few of them and sifted through the contents so that he would not have to enter into the small talk that was being discussed between Matilda, Ron and Mark. They were waiting for Andy, Joanne and Tom. Richard disliked having people in his office. He wanted to keep everyone thinking that to enter the office you needed to have a reason. If you were invited in, that was ok, but you had to be very important if you wanted to come in of your own free will. Using his office as a meeting place for the few people on the managers team was logical but he still didn't like it and usually tried to be a little distant.
Andy, Joanne and Tom walked through the door and he breathed an inner sigh of relief. They all said hello and quickly took the open chairs. When they had all quieted, Richard spoke.
"Alright, so last week at the meeting in New York I spoke with Donner and the other heads of the board and apparently they like us." Everyone in the room smiled. "Yes, it is obvious that they are trying to take over the world and not very happy with the rate of growth with Randley Financial Brokerage. We are growing but Merryl & Lynch has twice the assets that we do. The Swiss guys

are happy with us though because we have been gaining assets steadily, and they hope that our office will grow much more in the near future. All the other things we know as well but we will see." Richard looked down at his desk to a sheet of paper. To everyone it seemed as though they were points that he had written down to talk about, but it was actually a magazine cover.

"Joanne, how are we doing with this operational module thing?" Richard delegated all technology and computer things to Joanne.

"We are good. They are supposed to be done by Thursday, and we have seventy five percent of the office done." Joanne snapped her head over to Mark, "'Mark, I will print you out a list of who has and has not completed the module, and go around and make sure that everyone knows they must complete it."

"No problem."

Richard cleared his throat to take the attention of the floor. "Good. One thing that we need to start planning is this remodel for the office. We have about another five months if we want to get the building to pay for it according to our lease. Matilda, get on the phone and find out who we put the plans in with. I want to get this done as soon as possible if we can." Matilda nodded in affirmative.

Richard looked at Mark. "I got this email about the garage remodel. Do all the people with parking spaces know where they will be moved?"

Mark looked at Richard surprised, "Uh, I am not sure. I will let them know after the meeting." It was obvious to everyone in the room that Mark did not let anyone know, and was supposed to. "Can you forward me the email after the meeting also?"

With a grunt of annoyance Richard nodded. Mark looked down at his hands wondering why telling the people about the remodel fell in his hands.

Richard sat back a little. "Is there anything else that we have this morning?"

Joanne piped up. "I was talking to Hal this morning and he mentioned something." Hal was the regional manager of New England and Joanne tries her best to flirt with him as much as possible so she can get information.

"He said something about another office getting audited by the New York Stock Exchange." A groan came from Richard, Matilda and Ron. "Now, this doesn't mean that we are going to get one, but we haven't had an audit by them for two years, and we are due. I just suggest that we get all our files in order and make sure that we are ready if they waltz in here on Monday morning."

"Yes. An audit is just what we don't need right now. Although if we do get one I would rather it be from the stock exchange rather than our own team. The last time the exchange was here they didn't do anything except order Chinese food and dick around for a week in our board room."

"Yeah, and remember that one brunette girl who just flirted with Tom the whole time." Joanne looked over to Tom, who was smiling and blushing slightly. "All we had to do was team you up with her and she didn't do anything."

"Heh. It's a tough job."

"Alright. We will be ready if they come. Other than that, anything anyone has to say?"

"I got a new puppy this weekend." Matilda said cheerfully.

Everyone smiled and felt a little odd at the comment.

"My team went to the finals this weekend. We have another competition in two weeks." Ron said, attempting to put his own two cents in.

'I used my home hair-removal-electrolysis machine I bought off the QVC channel,' Mark thought silently.

Joanne, anxious to get back to her office said, "Well nothing happened to me. I need go print that module sheet though."

All understood the cue from Joanne and stood up and filed out of the room.

Richard looked at the chairs of the room, strewn about as though it were a party. He frowned and fixed them according to how they should be.

Chapter 6 - Characters

Brian Williams is about the size of a bear. He is giant, black and six feet four inches and just a little over three hundred pounds. He was a lineman for the New England Patriots, and after a successful career and three Super Bowl rings he decided to retire and enter into the professional world. He had majored in Business while in college and decided to start a path in investing. He uses his sports contacts to meet and help current professional athletes with their investments. The amount of people he knows in the area from football, baseball, basketball and hockey has helped him create a successful career.

Lawrence Knelling is a power broker in the office. He has spent many years in the office building his clients from retirement accounts for middle aged men to wealthy and influential families within the New England area. He has controlled his business in the office well enough that he is not ever bothered by Richard and instead of having a team of female assistants to take care of his needs he has three other brokers in the office that make very little and answer his phone and put orders in for him. He feels that the sound of a female voice is not very trustworthy. Most of the assistants in the office do not make very much money, and Larry noticed that in return for the poor payment most of the assistants do hardly any work.

His plan by bringing in the other brokers was that he would have three or maybe four white males in the office answering the phones for him and taking care of orders and wires. In return for doing the jobs of an assistant he would show them how to go about making a business. He would not have to pay them anything, since all brokers are on their own commission and they would work just as hard if not harder than a normal assistant.

Brian walks into the office at around 9:30 in the morning and grunts a hello to Nancy at the front desk. He usually comes in a little later than the rest of the brokers because he knows that there are not calls to make in the morning and he prefers to use his mornings for errands or to relax a bit before spending all day on the phone.

As he turns the corner and heads for his office he sees Lawrence coming the opposite way. Brian stiffens his back and smiles towards Larry. Larry looks up at the big man and his face forms a plastic grin as well. As they pass Lawrence mutters a good morning and Brian does likewise.

After they have crossed each other Lawrence thinks about how Brian is a token for the office and Brian questions in his mind how such a racist asshole can be so successful.

William Strindle comes into the office everyday around 10:30 a.m. He leaves around 2:00 p.m. William has not worked in the office for seven years. He retired from the profession after forty-five years. The result of his life after spending tireless years of cultivating his clients and schmoozing with the pseudo-riche is two divorces and no friends. William comes in to the office because he has nowhere else to go.

He is tolerated because of Richard's sense of loyalty and respect to the people who helped keep the office afloat over the years, as well as the sad truth that the office is lacking a decent amount of bodies to fill the desks. Personally, Richard dislikes the old retirees coming around and staying in the office but as long as they don't cause problems and make themselves invisible he can comfortably ignore them.

One day when William was feeling a little peckish he decided to make himself a bagel. After cutting the bread into halves he attempted to use the toaster. Unfortunately, he is not very keen on toaster science. After inspecting the toaster and its capabilities he decided to use the microwave instead. He was unsure as to the length of time needed to cook a bagel properly so he guesstimated about twelve minutes.

Around minute eight Mark happened to pass by the break room with the bagel BBQ, and made a mental note after getting a waft of the smoke that he should further instruct William how to properly cook whatever it was William was cooking. However, Mark reserved his intervention until after he had relieved himself.

Mid-piss Mark heard the fire alarm go off. With an admonishing shake of his head Mark finished headed for the break room.

When he entered he saw through the smoke that William had already doused the charred bagel halves with water and was proceeding to clean up the evidence.

"Hey William. Don't worry about it. I will go back to my desk and call security. Since the fire alarm went off I am sure they will want to check up here."

William kept on cleaning any blackened remains and nodded mutely.

Mark walked back to his desk and called security.

"Security, 100 Federal," answered a lady with an African accent.

"Hi, this is Mark on 27. You have a fire alarm that went off, right?"

"Yes. The fire department is on its way."

"Don't worry, you can call them off. It was just a bagel that caught on fire. There is no need to have the fire department come up here," Mark explained with chagrin.

"Uh, well, the fire department is automatic and we can't call them off. They will come and check the scene and then ok it."

"Alright, but there is really no need."

"I understand. They are in the building now and coming up," the lady paused for a moment, then said, "Did you say a bagel was on fire?" The lady said with utter disbelief.

Mark finished his conversation and started to walk towards reception so he could show the fire fighters to the scene of the fire. As he did, he noticed William on the other side of the office running towards the back elevator, in haste, with his jacket in his hand.

Mark raised an eyebrow and kept walking. When the fire fighters arrived Mark walked them to the break room while explaining the particulars of the emergency. The firefighters trudged along in their yellow suits and with their medical kits in hand and smiled and laughed at the false alarm. When they all entered the break room it was spotless of any evidence of a blaze except for a light haze in the air. They inspected the charred remains of a bagel strategically shoved at the bottom of the garbage can and verified the cause of the accident. The firefighters left with a wave and a caution about dabbling in the toasting arts and Mark sent an email to the office explaining succinctly, that there was no reason to raise alarm. All names pertaining to the cause of the emergency where omitted from the email.

The next day George Stapleton brought in a specially sized fire extinguisher that could be used for any further bagel emergencies.

Chapter 7 - Religion

The 'bullpen' of the office is the place where there is the most drama and the highest tension. The bullpen is a site of professional reincarnation. When a broker is new or comes to the company and has very few clients he is put in the bullpen. Also, when a broker is old, does not bring in very much money, and has no real reason to come to work he is usually asked to move to the bullpen. No one in the bullpen has an office. They all have a desk. There are no cubicles, so everyone can see you and hear you.

When brokers walk by they look at the people in the bullpen and remember it with nostalgia. The bullpen also acts as a symbol for most of the brokers. The struggle and fight to find prospective clients, and then the heartbreak when you lose them. The rejection that comes with almost every phone call; and then the eventual lack of feeling for the people you talk to over the phone.

After checking his mail box for any new shipments of the day, Mark walks back towards his desk. Coming through the hall he moves to the right side as someone comes the opposite way. As he steps to his right his foot sinks a little deeper in the padded carpet. To Mark it seemed that there was a divot or section of padding missing from underneath the fresh carpet that had just been installed. Mark cursed the office silently as he went on.

Coming around a corner and through the bullpen Mark saw that William Hamilton was on the phone. As soon as William came in to work he would sit down in his chair, type in his password and not take off his headset until it was time to leave. When he needed to get something off of the printer, he would unplug the headset, and walk to the printer with the headset firmly attached to his head. Then he would walk back and plug the headset back in. William waited for a very long time for the headset, and he took special care of it. He had special cleaners for the mouthpiece and a special foam phone buddy for his ear so that it would not get irritated. William likes his headset.

While walking by William's desk Mark nodded to William. William nodded back while still in mid conversation with a client.

Mark and William had a special conversation topic to talk about in the office; running a marathon. Mark had just ran his first marathon the month prior and it was William who had helped him find a ride to the race. It was the second marathon for William. At fifty-two William knew that he was getting old to be doing such long races, but he liked the challenge, and it gave him something to feel confident about.

After Mark passed William's desk he remembered that he had to look at a computer error at the desk directly behind William. Mark did an about face and walked to the work station. While at the desk and flicking the keys to figure out the root of the problem Mark looked at William's phone. The red light that normally indicates that the line is open was unlit. William did not have any open lines on his phone.

William still continued to be in conversation and was flicking through the programs on his own screen.

Mark cocked an eyebrow and went back to his work on the computer.

Geno Nanderi and Tom O'Brien are both veteran brokers in the office. They have both been in the office for more than forty years and in their time have made a decent amount of business, but never wanted to quit.

They both have given most of their business to another broker in the office, someone younger and more able to cater to the needs of the client. More able to search out information about the companies and stock on the computer. Also, younger brokers who are able to be in the office from nine until five.

Geno and Tom do not like to come in too early, they like to sleep in. They also like to leave after lunch because they can beat the traffic home.

Tom spends his day talking to the young brokers around him in the bullpen about all the companies he has seen rise and fall. Also, about the unexpected turns and pratfalls of the fools who try to make a million dollars.

Tom also likes to come to the office because he can take cigarette breaks. His wife does not know he smokes.

Geno doesn't like talking to the young brokers in the bullpen. He likes flirting with Noelle and Maria and Ly. Geno is not married, and most of his family doesn't live in Boston. The girls treat him like a cute teddy bear and in return he asks them occasionally if they want a real man.

A loud pitched beeping rings through the bullpen. It is coming from a watch on Geno's arm.

"Eeeeno! Dat's your alarm. Time to take your medicine." Noelle says in half baby talk and half normal.

"Alright kid, don't worry." Geno fumbles around his desk and suit pockets for his daily medication. The watch alarm is still going off.

"Geno, we need to find you a wife. I think that someone needs to take care of you." Ly says while painfully watching Geno look for his pills.

"I don't need one of those. Even if I did have one she wouldn't be as pretty as you."

Ly blushed slightly and a big smile lit her face. She likes that the old man openly taunts her and calls her beautiful.

Sitting in his chair, Geno fumbles through his pockets with great difficulty. His hands, elbows and shoulders bend in certain ways that make it seem as if he is a puppet on strings. With a final push of courage he reaches in his coat pocket that he placed over his chair and pulls out a small plastic baggie. There are three pills located inside, all different colors.

Geno places the baggie on his desk, and while attempting to catch his breath looks and concentrates on the bag.

"Noelle, which one am I supposed to take?"

"The pink one, Eeeeno."

Geno looks down and sees two pills in the bag that are a shade of pink. One is a bright fluorescent pink, and the other is a light pink similar to cotton candy.

"Pink bright or pink like Pepto Bismal?"

"Bright Eeeeeno."

Geno takes the pill and swallows it with a shot of water. After he places the plastic baggie back in his coat he looks at his computer screen, unable to remember what he was doing before he took his pill.

"You know when I was first selling bonds all we had to do was get buy a listing of the banks in the area and their rates and go to it on the phones. There were more private banks in those days. The cities big enough would open up their own bank, and of course the banks would want to compete with their interest rates so it was easy. In fact there were people who would do the research for you in those days, and all we would have to do is buy the sheet of the best interest rates and start calling. I would sell as far away as Kentucky or Wisconsin sometimes. It was easy. The clients would jump at the chance for three percent, sometimes four. It was easy pickens' back then. Of course now it is just as easy. I can search here on my computer for a list of bonds not just here in America, but also over in Europe or Asia. Just put in the interest rate I am looking for and call up the client. Put in the order in the computer and then it will be sent to the New York Stock Exchange within seconds. Back then we had to phone it in, and the order would be relayed by probably another three people and then get sent to the floor in New York. It took half a day to find out if the bonds were bought. Everything is so fast now." Tom looked on in space thinking about the amazing increase in speed that has happened to the business he has been in for over forty years. At first his mind went to the idea of computer and wires and electricity. That such information could be tapped out like morse code on his keyboard and sent like lighting hundreds of miles away. He thought about how he understands that it gets there, but he just doesn't understand how it all works. The thousands of little intricate pieces of machinery and lights and wires that connect everything. It all seems very complicated but, it works, because the clients end up with a bond that is bought in their name. A smile came over his face when he realized he had a very strong and complete trust in this thing that he didn't understand, because it works.

While Tom was midway through his historical narrative the new broker he was talking to had turned around and answered his phone. Within a couple of minutes the broker put in an order for a few hundred shares of a pharmaceutical company at the clients request and when he had finished he looked back to Tom and saw a serene look on his face. Tom was staring at the ceiling. The broker looked at the spot on the ceiling. He didn't see anything except white dry wall and a dark spot. He suspected the spot was from a leaking pipe. The broker looked back at Tom.
"So, what was that about bonds Tom."
Tom broke out of his trance and looked at the broker with a face that showed worry. Tom felt fear again, about not knowing something. His memory played tricks on him constantly, and sometimes he would be in a room or hallway and forget why he was there. He did not know why this broker was asking him about bonds.
"I have made my business on bonds Jake." The broker looked as if he was going to correct Tom, but decided not to. "Always make your business on the investments you can trust. The millionaires are one in a million. One in a billion. Don't fool yourself about how to make it in this business Jake. It is hard. But if you try, you can make a good decent living. Always keep your nose clean, and never get greedy." Tom ended his suggestion with a wink and smile.

3:11 p.m.
Swiveling around in his chair, Geno looks around to the girls typing away last minute wires and the new young rookie brokers that are chatting away on the telephone. He turns his chair facing his desk and looks at his computer monitor. He squints slightly, thinking to himself that he needs to change his prescription again. The monitor is full of colors and lines and letters. He can't see what they mean unless he puts his head directly in front of the monitor. The chart on the screen is sloping upwards at the end. He thinks this means that the value of the chart has gone up. That makes him happy. Geno likes to see things increase in value. If there is one thing he has learned, it is that the value always increases in the market. All it needs is time. There will always be moments of busts or depressions, but the market always grows. Like a tree. Surrounded by other trees. In a great forest. And, America is a great big sequoia in this forest. The biggest sequoia. Like, one of those old growth sequoias that you can drive through in California. He is part of that. He feels like a little branch or twig on this great big tree.
He looks away from his monitor. He glances over to Ly's desk and sees that there is a pack of cigarettes and a lighter. He contemplates the lighter. He wonders what would happen if the forest caught on fire. A giant forest fire, like

they have in California. His heart starts to beat a little faster. Geno thinks that it is time to leave for the day.

Geno stands up slowly with his hands on his desk so he can keep his balance. He looks back at the suit jacket that is hung on the back of the chair. He grabs it off of the chair and puts one arm through. As he brings the other sleeve around he tries to put his arm through, but can't quite bend it all the way.

"Hey Eeeeeno. Are you headed out?" Noelle says in her baby talk.

"Yeah kid. I am going to be off in a second."

Geno is fumbling around with his jacket, trying to get the sleeve to cooperate. Mark walks by the desk on his way to fix a computer when Noelle asks, "Hey Mark, can you help Geno with his jacket?"

Suddenly aware of the other people around him Mark answers, "Uh, yeah sure. No problem."

Mark straightens out the other side of Geno's jacket and helps his arm through. Geno looks at him and with a red face from the physical effort gives him a nod and says, "Thanks kid."

Geno picks up his briefcase and newsie cap and heads on out towards the elevators.

"Bye, Eeeeeno," Noelle says sweetly.

"Bye Geno," Maria says with a smile.

Ly runs after Geno with something wrapped in a paper towel. "Geno don't forget the bread I made for you."

"No kid, I wouldn't forget it. See you tomorrow."

"Bye," Ly says lovingly.

Walking slowly and with a gait that showed his despondency, Mark headed towards his desk. Matilda was up at Joanne's office; there was one more hour left until five o'clock. Mark was alone and waiting for the time to be up. Looking at his screen he opened Microsoft word. The animated paper clip icon appeared in the bottom right, and Mark closed it, while feeling nothing but malevolence.

Mark looked at his computer screen and started to write. "Take ten minutes of your day. A simple ten minutes that you don't normally mind or that seems to be filled with something nonsensical like picking which pair of socks will feel fluffier or which glass might be cleaner to drink from. These moments of banality make me feel queasy. In fact they make me want to sit on my toilet and shit a little. With more introspection as to my day I realize that it is filled with these incendiary fecal producers. Maybe I have the hope that my day will be filled with meaning and some semblance of usefulness. It just doesn't quite seem like that is happening.

I wonder if this is why people start drinking?"

Chapter 8 - Savior

Mark was sitting at his desk wondering when the Verizon representative was going to show up.

The Randley Financial Brokerage company headquarters in some other state let him know that they would arrive at the office between nine in the morning and four in the afternoon.
While waiting for something to happen Mark started searching through the Muppets website. At first it was to see which characters were actually Muppets. Mark had always felt slightly unsure which characters he could remember as being part of the Muppets and which could be part of Sesame Street. After an hour, Mark attempted to start looking for the Muppet with the most hair. Then the Muppet with the largest fuzz to hair ratio.
He decided it was Fozzie Bear.
In the background he heard a faint noise like a fan or air conditioner malfunctioning. He made a note on a piece of paper that it was one more thing to check out. After putting the paper aside he decided to wait until someone brought it to his attention.
Paul Rosen ran by his desk in a worried half walk half run.
"Do you know CPR?" He asks as he continues past hurriedly.
"Uh, Yeah," Mark answered questioningly.
"Go back there and help William." Paul pointed to the direction of where William Strindle normally sits.
Mark stood up and walked quickly to where William sits. Mark had not actually been formally introduced to William, but knew who he was. He still felt the need to ask his name before he spoke to him.
Mark came to the spot where William Strindle was sitting in his chair and noticed the wheezing noise that was coming out of William's throat. Mark came up to William and started to see if William was conscious or not.
"Hello, how are you feeling (looking at Kyle Sullivan to the right for the name. Kyle mouths 'William') William?"
Mark took his left hand in his right and gently put pressure. His eyes were rolled slightly back in his head, but the lids were slightly ajar, so it gave the impression that he was awake.
"William. How are you? Are you feeling any pain or is there anything that doesn't feel right?" Mark said in a calm tone.
William gave no verbal response and instead did a very sudden and alarming intake of breath. After a minute of observing his bodies struggle with life Mark brought William down to the floor with the help of Kyle and Rebecca Bonnair.

His jacket was off and solely a shirt was on his torso.
Someone had called 911 and said they suggested rubbing his body and helping circulation. Seeing his face and lips start to turn a shade of purple and blue Mark decided to start rubbing his chest and stomach to try and help. William still had a faint pulse and his lungs were still fighting to breathe about every twenty seconds. Soon after William was on the floor that stopped. His face was a dark purple hue, and it looked like he was going into cardiac arrest.
Doug Carey was there and kneeled down after Mark said that it was time to start with CPR. Doug kneeled next to his body.
"I am afraid I will break his ribs."
"It might happen. But it's better to be alive with a broken rib than be dead."
"You take the body."
Mark positioned himself next to the torso so he could do a thrust that would supply the circulation needed.
Doug went next to the mouth and prepared to breathe into the aging man.
"Ready?" Mark asked.
Doug nodded.
Mark counted five repetitions and then told Doug to breathe.
"Don't force, but be firm. Tilt the head back. Make sure his tongue is not in the way."
Mark and Doug felt no life going into William, but they continued to assist him. Building security had sent a guy up with a defibrillator. He kneeled a distance away from the body and fumbled nervously with the kit. Doug and Mark looked at each other, stopped for a second thinking the man could help, then started with CPR again.
The paramedics came a minute later and took over.
Mark explained the beginning of the situation and sat on a desk nearby if they needed help. Mark was feeling a giant surge of adrenaline and while they took over it all seemed very quick.
The paramedics left. Mark cleaned up after them and took the urine stained chair out to be trashed.
Afterwards there were many women circling the halls in disbelief and shock. Mark sat at his desk, silently hoping that walls would form up around it so that he could get a few moments of peace instead of constant questions from people roaming the office asking anyone around what had happened and trying to get a glimpse of the whole story.
Mark noticed that he had unchecked emails. One was a notification that there was a printer jammed on the twenty-eighth floor. He told Matilda where he was going and headed on up to try and fix the printer as slowly as possible.

Chapter 9 - Greater Expectations

Slowly, Mark walks to the subway station after coming out of the Boston Sports Club. He tiredly looks up into the sky and sees a faint trace of sunset through the downtown buildings. The air is crisp and there is a slight breeze running through the buildings. He pulls the hood of his sweater over his head and moves on to the subway station.

The financial area of Boston closes down after five o'clock. People rush out of the buildings and by seven o'clock; the entire area is barren and has a complete lack of life. It is a nice time to walk through the buildings because there isn't a massive hoard of people rushing against you or bumping into you.

Slowly, enjoying the weather Mark walks towards Boston Common. As he steps out from the last building to the giant grassy knoll, he breathes in the deep autumn air. He steps into the tunnel for the Green Line and slips his T-pass through the scanner.

Mark usually takes the Orange line home because it is much quicker. The Orange line is a strictly underground subway, where the Green Line is underground part of the way and then run on surface streets for the last few miles. Boston is a congested mess of traffic and confusion on the streets and the Green Lines are always the slowest of all the Boston Subway routes.

Mark prefers the Green line because they go past three major colleges in Boston and the college girls are much prettier than the working class women who huddle on the Orange line. However, Mark much prefers gaining a half hour of sleep in the morning by taking the Orange line.

Stepping slowly up and seating himself by a window, Mark starts to nod off after another long week of work. It is Friday, and Mark doubled his workout at the gym so that he would make up for not going to the gym on Tuesday. One of his friends and roommate, Ajay, had a gig at a bar in Allston a few miles away. Mark is dedicated to help Ajay and support him whenever he needs it. Mark gladly gave up his few hours of relaxation and peace working out so that he could help Ajay load up his truck and then set up the instruments at the bar. Mark thought about the gig of Ajay's and was slightly annoyed. Ajay is one of the people Mark is closest to. He feels that Ajay is a brother and treats him as he would family. However, over the years since Mark met Ajay in college he learned how Ajay can have terrible mood swings, be very sensitive to criticism and generally suffer from a severe case of Attention Deficit Disorder.

In the back of his mind as his eyes were closing and he was starting to dream, Mark felt like there was something that he was supposed to remember and do, but did not care very much about it. Sleep was all that he wanted and felt was important.

As if on autopilot, Mark's brain told him to wake up. He was at the last stop of the Green E Line, and picked up his bag and stepped out onto the pavement. He started the walk up towards the Veteran Hospital and towards the street where he lived.

Climbing up the steps, he made his way into the apartment and put his suit and gym bag down on the bed. He only felt tired, but knew that he should eat something, otherwise he would feel very hungry later.

Downing some milk, yogurt and a banana he started to place some fish in a pan to cook. Mark heard noisy footsteps coming down the stairs from the second floor. They sounded like dress shoes the way they stiffly hit the creaking wood floor boards. Ajay was the only one in the house who constantly wore wing tip dress shoes, so Mark figured it was him.

Ajay rounded the corner dressed in slacks and a colored dress shirt. He gave Mark a look up and down and then cocked an eye brow. "Dude, are you going to be ready? We leave in like five minutes."

Mark looked over at Ajay and racked his brain for what Ajay was talking about. He decided that it had to be something in which he must dress up, but couldn't remember what it was.

"Man, I hate to say this, but where am I supposed to go tonight?"

"Dude, we are going to the FABRIC concert for HMS." Somewhere on the right side of Mark's brain synapses were firing and it gave a very warm and whirling sensation to his head. Also the decoding of the acronyms were a starting to unravel as well. FABRIC stood for Featured African and Black Roots in Culture and HMS stood for Harvard Medical School. Ajay was actually in the dental program at Harvard, but it is a joint program with the medical school for the first two years. Living with four students in medical school Mark had gotten used to the acronyms and only occasionally asked for clarification. For the most part Mark didn't care, and ignored his roommates when they started excitedly talking about the new function of the liver they learned or how the effect of a certain drug would isolate a virus in the pancreas but leave every other organ unharmed.

Mark sat down and contemplated going to the show with his minimal amount of energy. "Man, I don't think I can make it this time. I am just out of juice."

"Dude, don't puss out, you can come. You got the energy. Dude, Sirena is going to be a belly dancer. Doesn't that make you want to come?"

Sirena was a dental classmate of Ajay's. Mark had had a crush on her from the moment he met her. She was not only a breathtakingly beautiful half American and half Spanish girl, but she was from California like Mark, and had a very laid back and relaxed feel that he found comfortable and nostalgic of his home.

"Dude, I am just too tired. I really just want to crash out and sleep for a few days."

"Dude, you are such a puss. Fine, be a little bitch and just stay on the couch and sleep. Man you used to go out and have fun, now that you work you just puss out whenever there is a party. You need to start getting out more. I swear man, you are getting old."

Mark looked up at Ajay and knew that it was true. He was starting to act like his parents, and he was only twenty-three. Mark started a defense. "I went with you to your gig on Tuesday."

"Yeah, you did. But you just ordered a beer and were half asleep in the corner."

I could have been asleep if you and the band didn't pump up the volume on the speakers so loud, Mark thought.

"Yeah, but I was there and I was talking with some of your classmates. I get out on the weekends sometimes."

"Dude face it, you are old and boring."

"Just wait. Once you get out of school it will be the same."

"No way man. I am going to be a dentist. I am going to work a nine to four, get three days off a week, and make a buttload of cash. I will still do gigs on the weekends, and have a band."

"Yeah dude. Um, not really. You will make money yeah, but you will have to buy in to a practice and join a HMO if you want to make the cash you are thinking about. You will have to spend your free time practicing new skills, especially if you want to specialize. And you might think that you will have time for a band, but dude, after all day on your feet talking to people, or I should say asking questions and hearing gargles as answers, you are not going to want to spend more time playing music, you will be tired and want a drink. Face it, what you got right now, with school, is freedom. You can study and practice and not have much to do. What you have now is the most freedom with your time you are going to have for a long time."

Ajay looked at Mark with deep eyes for a second, and then walked over to the fridge and took out the milk. He poured himself a glass and said, "Harsh man, harsh."

Mark stood up and went back to cooking his fish.

Ajay sat down with a cookie he took from a tin and said, "Hey, how did you like the gig on Tuesday?"

Mark thought about his words carefully. He knew how sensitive Ajay could be about any criticism, and how quickly Ajay would rise to defend himself as well as argue any statements made. Mark thought about the best way to tell his friend how he felt that his songs were sad, since they were almost all about a girl he had broken up with three years ago and how on stage Ajay had no idea how loud the speakers were in the audience of the small bar. Mark still didn't understand why Ajay needed to have a PA sound system with speakers that were twice as big as Ajay himself.

"I like the groove of the band, but I thought it was a little loud. Dude, can you guys get smaller speakers for small places like that." Mark felt ok since he had partially told the truth.

"Naw man, the speakers are fine. That is what you need for gigs like that. Then the groove gets flooded into the whole place. Everyone gets bumpin' an' movin' with the whole thing." Ajay stood up and started dancing a little to a song in his head. Mark looked over and couldn't help but love the little Indian guy.

The fish in the pan was ready to be eaten and Mark felt so hungry that he decided not to use a plate. He placed the pan down on a hot pad on the table and started to eat the fish with a fork.

After a few bites he got a craving for vegetables and went to the fridge to get a handful of uncooked broccoli. He put a few in his mouth and went back to the table and placed the rest beside his pan of cooked fish.

Ajay walked into the living room and sat down at the piano. He started playing a few chords he had been fiddling with for the past week. He would play them repeatedly using new rhythms and tempos. To Mark it sometimes sounded like it was a slow country western tune, sometimes it was very fast and scary and sometimes it sounded like it was one of the songs from Grease.

As if the piano was a dinner bell calling upstairs, Shawn and Nancy came down from their rooms. Rounding the corner, Mark saw they too were dressed in dress pants and shirts. Shawn had a tie on as well.

Mark felt a slight cringe in his stomach after seeing his friends in the dress clothes. Mark disliked suits and dress clothes. He found suits be uncomfortable and ties to be a pointless accessory of cloth.

For his job Mark had to wear a suit and tie every day. This was something that Mark found to be nonsensical and stupid since his job as the gopher of the office meant that he was constantly moving around the office and moving heavy objects. There were few things that Mark found as uncomfortable as a thin layer of sweat mixed with the thin wool fabric of his suit pants. It would itch, the fabric would harden and taken on a new form, and by the end of the day Mark felt like he smelled like a sheep.

Seeing his friends dressed in the clothes made him feel sad. He bowed his head and looked into his pan of fish and shoveled more into his mouth. The presence of the dress clothes soiled the sanctuary of his home. It made him feel depressed, like somehow his job had followed him home and seeped in through the cracks like a dense fog. He felt his heart constrict and wanted to cry.

Mark then also realized that he was probably very tired from exercising, and that was why he was feel such a strong abhorrence for the dress clothes that he didn't like.

"Dude, aren't you coming?" Shawn asked.

"Nah, I don't think I am going to make it tonight. I am just too tired."

"Come on, you know you want to. There are going to be belly dancers," Nancy said with a wink.

"Nah, all that I see in my future is a couch and a book."

"Come on man, I am going to be doing my hip hop moves, you know you want to see me bust it out," Nancy said while starting to sing Britney Spears, 'Oops I Did It Again,' and moving her body in a hip hop dancing sort of fashion.

Nancy has very little control over her coordination. It is quite an amazing fact that she can move her legs in the morning and actually arrive to school.

Mark watched Nancy dance in the kitchen and realized even more than before that he did not want to go to the concert.

After finishing his food Mark put the pans in the sink and walked to his room. He changed his clothes and took up a book. It was a tour guide of Mexico. He walked to the living room and laid out on the couch.

Shawn walked through the living room towards the stairwell. He looked over at Mark and said, "Planning the trip again? Where are you going to go in Mexico?"

"I am not sure. I am just going to go in the direction that I feel like. Now I am just trying to read some maps and get a feel for the routes that are open."

"When are you going to go?"

"I don't know. As soon as I get enough money. Maybe next June."

"And where are you going to go again?"

"As many places as I can. Mexico, Cuba, Caribbean, South America…"

Shawn smiled and said, "Dude, that is so cool."

Mark smiled and looked back down and put his nose in his book.

Nancy turned and started for the stairwell and then turned back. "Hey, how did things go with that guy you did CPR on?"

Mark looked up. "Oh, well, it went alright. He regained consciousness after a few days. I heard that he is out of the hospital. There weren't any broken bones or anything, just some bruises. All in all he is going to be ok."

"That is good. I still can't believe that out of all the people in this house you are the only one who has actually saved someone. I mean, we're all in med school."

Mark smiled and nodded. As Shawn turned and went to the stairwell Mark said, "Yeah, I know it seems odd. But you know what the weird thing was?"

"No, what?"

"It was how people acted afterwards. About a week after it happened his wife and daughter from New York came in the office and wanted to meet the people who were there and had helped. It was nice to meet them and explain what happened and all. They actually gave me a bottle of wine and a card explaining their thanks. I was jazzed. I mean I didn't expect anything, but the weird thing was how the people in the office reacted. I mean a lot were really critical about what the family did. One person came up and asked me what they gave me. I

told them a bottle of wine and a note. Then the person said, 'You saved his life and all that they gave you was a bottle of wine and a note? God, how cheap. If you would have saved my life I would have given you anything you wanted. My lord. Only a bottle of wine? Now that is what you call a blue-nose.'
I was so appalled dude. I mean, I did what I hope anybody would have done. But the people in the office were really critical about how this guy said thanks. Don't get me wrong, I mean it would be cool to be given a million dollars for doing something as simple as CPR, but I didn't expect anything. I can't imagine the shock that the dude went through after all that happened to his body."
Shawn nodded silently and thought for a second about what to say. "I guess that the people in the office just expected more from a guy who just had his life saved. I mean what kind of a gift do you give someone for saving your life?"
"I know man, but it was just odd the way people jumped all over him for only giving me a bottle of wine. I guess I just expected more of them, you know."
Shawn nodded and said, "Yeah, I get ya."
Mark put his nose back in his book.
Shawn headed upstairs to his room.

Chapter 10 - A Waste

5:00 p.m.

Boston had a slight chill coming into the city. It was early December and there were still small mounds on the sidewalks of ice left over from the first snow storm of winter.

A block away from the Boston Sports Club Tom and Mark bumped into one another. They both went to the same gym after work, and would sometimes walk together and make small talk.

Entering into the locker room they changed into their clothes for exercising. Tom looked down at the dress socks Mark had on and commented that they would soon become stirrups. Mark nodded in agreement. His socks had two giant holes where the toes were. In fact, two toes were sticking out of the socks. Tom left the locker room to start his work out and Mark followed shortly afterward.

Mark sat down on the electric bike and started pedaling. He rotated through a routine of running and biking and the stair master.

Looking around Mark noticed the large amount of young people in the gym. It seemed odd to see so many. It was as if they were all still in college. He figured there weren't very many older people because they had more responsibilities or maybe a family to take care of.

Mark looked ahead and saw Tom jogging on the treadmill ten feet away. Mark searched out the crowd to see if there was anybody else that he knew there.

Out of the corner of his eye he saw Tom falter. Mark looked over in time to see Tom lose his balance with his right foot on the treadmill. This was not an unusual thing to see, but Mark kept watching him.

Mark saw Tom rapidly lose his balance on his right leg and then his left started to collapse as well. Tom started to tumble down to the belt of the treadmill and then was thrown off onto the floor behind it.

Mark lunged off his bike and to the side of Tom. Putting his hand on Tom and talking to him he tried to see what was the matter.

Tom was on his back and his muscles were tensing and trying to fight something inside him. Mark looked at his face, asking Tom what was the matter and where the pain was. Tom was not speaking and instead started to make a groaning sound like he had been wounded. Mark saw the color drain from his face and his pupils were contracting until they were the size of pin heads.

Not sure what to do Mark took Tom's arm in his hand and looked into his eyes and tried to see if he could understand anything that might be saying. Mark put his hand on Tom's wrist and looked for a pulse. Tom's heart was beating as fast as a machine gun and Mark knew that something inside Tom was very wrong.

He looked into Tom's face and tried to make out some solution but was drawing a blank.

By this time people had surrounded Mark and Tom in curiosity and to see if there was anything they could do. Someone had gone to the desk to get them to call an ambulance.

A short Indian lady came through the crowd and kneeled next to Tom. She identified herself as a doctor and asked Mark who Tom was and what had happened.

Mark told her everything that had transpired.

"His name is Tom Stevenson. I work with him down the street. He was on the treadmill for about five minutes and then he collapsed. His face is losing color and pupils are contracted. I don't have a count on his pulse but it is very rapid like a machine gun. He has a recent history of blacking out during his basketball games on the weekend, but there isn't a set pattern of when it happens. He has been through extensive testing to figure out what the cause is, but it is not known."

"Is he on any medication?"

"I don't know."

"Go and get his bag and look for any medication or pills."

Mark and a staff member raced to the locker room to look for Tom's bag. They found it and looked inside for pills or some type of medication. They found it and raced back to the doctor with the backpack in hand.

The doctor looked at the pills and said, "Beta blockers. That wouldn't do anything like this."

By this time two staff members had started doing CPR on Tom and the doctor was on the phone with the ambulance telling them what to prepare for. The siren of an ambulance was getting closer.

The manager of the gym came over to Mark and asked about what had happened. Mark told him everything that had gone on up to the moment. The manager listened and left to show the paramedics where the situation was.

Mark looked at the doctor and Tom and tried to think of something to do. He rifled through Tom's bag and found his cell phone. Possibly Tom's parents would know more about Tom's situation and could help with information. Looking through the phone list Mark spotted one name that said Dad. He pressed the dial button.

Mark waited nervously.

"Hey AD, what's going on?" The voice was warm and fatherly.

"Hello Mr. Stevenson, my name is Mark Harmon. I work with Tom at Randley Financial Brokerage and I am here with him in the gym. I wanted to let you know that he has blacked out again and that he is unconscious, but people are taking care of him right now. I am also calling to see if you know anything more about his condition. Did they find the cause of it, or maybe a reason for why it happened?"

"Uh…um, no they haven't found the reason yet. Is he alright? What is going on?"

"He was on the treadmill and he collapsed. Right now he is on the floor and he is not conscious, but there are people with him right now taking care of him."

"OK, OK. Wow, this hasn't happened in a couple of months, the doctors cleared him for going back and exercising."

"I know sir, Tom told us at work," Mark said. Mark thought about who he could talk to for more information and maybe to learn more about Tom's condition.

"Mr. Stevenson, do you know who Tom's roommates are here in Boston? I want to let them know where he is and what has happened."

"Um, yeah. We met one of them, his name is Irv. Tom just moved into a new house, so we don't know who most of the new people are."

"OK, Irv. I will let him know. I will call you and make sure that you know what is going on and where Tom is going, alright?"

"Yes, yes Mark. Thanks so much. Thanks."

Mark looked around at a crowd that had gathered in the gym to watch what was happening to Tom. Mark saw a beautiful tall blonde girl looking at him. It was Kate, a girl who worked on the other side of the office at Randley Financial Brokerage. She walked over to him and he explained what had happened.

The next hour was a lot of moving and talking and explaining and waiting. Police came in and asked questions, got information and took Mark and Kate to the hospital.

Mark and Kate were brought in to the waiting room. After a few minutes they were brought into the sitting room which was closed off from the rest of the emergency room. The nurse told them that the doctors would be right in.

Mark thought about why the doctors would be right in. Shouldn't they be working to save Tom?

Chairs lined the walls of the room and Mark sat on one side and Kate another. After a few minutes Mark switched sides and sat next to Kate. They were both very quiet.

After a few minutes two men in scrubs and long white coats came in. They both were thin and wiry men in their early forties who looked like they drank too much coffee and didn't sleep enough. They pulled up chairs and were sitting across from Kate and Mark.

"I am doctor Reynolds."

"And I'm Doctor Rosenbaum."

"You are both friends of Tom?" Doctor Reynold asked them.

Kate nodded silently and Mark said, "Yeah. We are friends and we work with him as well."

Doctor Reynolds looked at Mark and Kate and said, "Well, I am very sorry to tell you this, but Tom has passed away."

Kate took one of Mark's hands and with the other she covered her face and started to cry.

The room was very dead, except for Kate's crying.

Mark was the first to break the silence.

"Well…shit."

Doctor Reynolds nodded and said, "Yeah. It is one of those sad moments."

Kate spoke up pleadingly, "But he was so young and such a good athlete. I can't believe this would happen to him. He is only twenty six."

Doctor Reynolds spoke about the condition he was in when he came to the hospital. After finding that Mark was there when it happened initially he questioned Mark about what had happened in the first moments.

When the Doctors had enough information they explained to Mark and Kate that they could stay in the room for as long as they wanted, and there were grief counselors at the hospital if they needed to talk to someone.

Mark remembered that Tom had parents and made a comment about how he should probably give them a call.

"Don't worry about that. We have people who will take care of notifying his parents. Don't worry about that," Doctor Reynolds said reassuringly.

After a few more minutes of talking to the nurses and deciding it was time to go, Mark and Kate made their way out of the hospital and to their homes.

During everything that had happened Boston had turned cold and windy. The sky was dark when Mark started walking back to his apartment.

When he entered the apartment he put his things back down on the bed and started staring a hole into his pillow. He felt exhausted and wanted to sleep, but was not sure if he could. Looking at his pillow he started thinking about his ex-girlfriend from college. It provided some comfort.

He went upstairs to Ajay's room and left a note on his computer. Then Mark got under the covers and closed his eyes. He was not asleep, instead he was thinking about all the superstitions or myths he had ever heard about the recently deceased.

The feeling that Tom might be in the room hanging around was what occupied his mind the most. He remembered that he should call Matilda and tell her what happened.

He found his phone and explained to her what had happened. He said he would be in to work early and they could talk about how they would tell the office. Mark went back under the covers and started to give way to sleep.

At some point Mark heard his door creak open and Ajay walked in. Mark turned on a light and saw that he had a tired look on his face. Mark asked Ajay how he was and Ajay went into a long explanation of his day and difficulties with creating a wax tooth. Ajay felt a lack of confidence about his abilities, and didn't know what to do.

Mark was silent throughout the whole speech and eventually Ajay asked Mark how he was.

"Well, my day sucked. Do you remember Tom who we went to the Victor Wooten concert with? Well, today at the gym he collapsed and after people trying to save him and going to the hospital he passed away."

Ajay sat in silence. Unsure of what to say he leaned over and gave Mark a hug. Mark explained all he could about the night, and especially anything he knew about Tom. Ajay listened and let Mark talk.

After a while Mark was starting to yawn, and Ajay saw it was time for him to sleep. Mark looked at the door after his friend left.

After a minute he turned out the light and turned into his bed and slept.

Next morning Mark woke up early. The air felt colder than normal and he tried to take a shower as long as possible so that he could get the cold feeling out of his skin.

He walked towards the giant red building and wondered how long the day was going to be.

Walking towards his desk he noticed that Matilda was in her office. He put his bag down on his desk and walked in.

"How ya feeling?" Matilda said. She was slumped in her chair and had heavy bags under her eyes.

"Oh you know, could be better. But I am OK."

Matilda looked down at her desk and breathed deeply but inaudibly. Mark took a seat opposite from the desk. Matilda and Mark looked at each other and moved their mouths in half smiles.

"I can't even imagine what today is going to be like," Matilda said breaking the silence.

Mark nodded his head and looked out the window to another building across Boston. To Mark they all seemed like figurines from the twenty-seventh floor. They were all something unreal and really just props for any clients that came in so that the office looked a bit more professional.

"Did you get a hold of Richard last night?" Mark asked.

"Yeah, I got him at his hotel in New York. He is going to be here as soon as he can after his meeting at noon."

Matilda went to click on an email that had just came into her inbox, then sat back in her chair.

"So, tell me what happened," she said coolly.

Mark recanted the whole story. He left out the memories he had of Tom lifeless, colorless on the floor of the gym and in the stretcher at the hospital. He told her about calling his parents, about the doctors, about Kate, about walking home. He apologized to Matilda for calling so late.

"No, don't worry about it. I never sleep anyways. Too many kids, they all either keep you up by making noise or by making you worry where they are. Katie had her cast party last night, so I watched the news and made sure there wasn't any sudden stories about drunk kids driving off the road."

"Yeah. I didn't get much sleep last night either. I felt exhausted, but still just couldn't get my eyes closed."

"I imagine it must have been hard."

Matilda talked a little bit more about Katie and Mark asked about how Charlie was doing in football.

"You know Peter had him last weekend and decided to take him instead to a boat show. Not only that, but Charlie was going to sleep over at a friend's house and his father decided to cancel that and instead take him to his girlfriends for a dinner. The only people that were there were other attorneys. I can't fucking believe that the guy would do such a thing. Charlie needs to be with his friends and how is he going to get better at playing the sport if he isn't there to play the game?"

Mark had heard many complaints from Matilda about her ex-husband. At first Mark just listened because he understood that his boss needed someone to vent to. After a while, hearing the weekly escapades about her ex Mark felt pity for her and her kids. He realized that he was only hearing one side of the story, but if half was true, the guy was a dead beat.

"I swear I would pay someone with a lead pipe if I could get away with it," Matilda said in frustration.

Mark thought for a moment. He felt like making a joke. "Well, it seems that I have the touch of death right now. I mean first Strindle and now Tom. All you need to do is bring him in the office and I will see what I can do."

Matilda and Mark laughed a bit, but nervously because it was a bad joke.

"You know I just might do that."

"Do you want me to write a letter to the office?" Mark said calmly.

"No, that's ok. I will do it. You have done enough already," Matilda said with a caring voice. "If you want to leave at any time today it is OK. Just let me know and I will cover for you."

"No, that's alright. I will be able to stay the whole day. Besides, I wouldn't want the place to fall apart."

"Hey, I used to do your job before you were here. I showed Tom how to do it. I can still do a few things, don't worry."

"Heh, yeah I know. But don't worry, I will be here."

Shortly before eight o'clock in the morning Matilda sent out an email to the office. It was short, but to the point.
"Dear everyone,
Last night Tom Stevenson passed away. He collapsed while at the gym and was taken to MGH shortly afterward. We will make any information as to any funeral arrangements available as soon as possible."

At this time in the office there were not very many people logged in to their computer. Those that were called Matilda immediately and asked if it was true. Mark looked at the email and imagined how many people would come in to work today, log in to their computer, and read an email about their coworker's death.
The morning was filled with people calling Matilda and walking by her desk to ask about what happened. Mark answered her phone and talked to the people as best he could. He knew that he was the one that had the story, and that Matilda didn't really want to answer questions from all of the people about Tom.
Mark told the story for four hours. Different people came by and all asked about what happened? Where? How?
They asked about last words, about where he was from, about his family. They made arguments against his death like, 'He was only twenty six,' or, 'He was in perfect shape,' or, 'But he was such a nice kid.'

At one o'clock Mark wandered into Matilda's office.
"Hey Miss, I think I am going to go get some lunch."
"Yeah, go ahead. Things have quieted down a bit anyways."
Mark walked out of the building and walked for a while. After going past restaurants and delicatessens Mark found that he was either not very hungry or didn't feel like eating. In the distance he saw a hot dog vendor next to the Downtown Crossing T-stop.
Since he was a kid he always asked for hot dogs and fruit salad for his birthday dinner when his Mom asked him. He went up to the vendor and ordered two. He had him put on ketchup and mustard. After paying he walked to the little park near the post office. The small patch of green grass always looked odd since it was surrounded by huge geometric mountains of steel and glass and concrete.
He sat down and bit into the hot dog. He knew that he was eating a hot dog, but it didn't taste like anything in his mouth.
He looked up at the buildings, but they were all very far away and looked fake like figurines.
Mark stood up, threw away his hot dogs and walked back to the office.

Chapter 11 - Harness

After bringing out the suitcase from under the bed Mark saw that a film of dust had accumulated on top of it. He poked his finger in the soft mess and made a happy face.
He had put enough clothes for a week on his bed as well as the presents for his family. All together it looked neat and organized. The clothes were neatly folded and everything was packed away so that nothing could be harmed during the flight. Mark disliked the look of the order. It reminded him of someone with obsessive compulsive disorder. He took out part of the shirts and laid them so that they would get wrinkled with the weight of the other clothes. This made him feel a bit better.

Ajay poked his head around the frame to Mark's door. "Hey dude, when is your flight?"
"It is at one. I should be going in about an hour."
"Cool. I am off to go study for my test, so I just want to say goodbye and merry Christmas." Ajay walked towards Mark with arms outstretched.
"Thanks man. Have a good time with your family too."
"Yeah, you know it. I am looking forward to going back to LA. The weather is supposed to be nice, and my sister is going to be back from Ecuador. It will be nice to see her."
"Yeah."
"Alright, I am off. Have a good flight."
"Thanks. I will see you in a couple of weeks."
"Lates."
"Lates."
Mark heard the door close behind Ajay, and he had a strong urge not to leave his room. He tried to picture what the next week with his family was going to be like. Seeing his mother and talking about recipes and how things were with the house. Also, talking to his sister and making her jealous about how many times he saw the Boston Red Sox play this year; which is her favorite team. Possibly going to dinner with his brother and hearing about how he is doing with his SCUBA diving and if he is closer to changing jobs. And trying to dodge his father and not get cornered into a conversation about Mark's future in the company.
It was going to be nice and quaint for about two or three days, then it will become boring. Mark does not keep in touch with kids he grew up with and has no wish to seek them out. Mark can ask to borrow his sister's car, but there is only so much driving he can do before it becomes boring as well.

He has already brought five books and knows that with all the free time he will probably finish them in three days.

Mark thinks about how much TV his family watches and almost becomes sad and knowing that at about seven o'clock his family will be shut off from the world in dedication to their programs.

Looking at his suitcase, Mark is tempted to put the clothes back and just stay in his room and apartment for a week reading his books and renting movies.

It might almost be better.

Stepping off the plane Mark felt a great pressure on his bladder. He walked as quickly as possible down the aisle and into the terminal. Just as he got out of it he saw the Men's room. He darted in and relieved himself.

Walking out of the men's room he saw his father standing directly in front of the doorway. His father was tall and had thin muscular legs and skinny arms. All Mark's childhood his father had been devout at going to the gym, but focused all his time on the stair master and doing sit ups. His father now had a slight paunch. His skin was also a color of dark brown from laying by a pool deck whenever he got a chance. Wearing jeans and a white parka, Mark thought his father looked curiously odd with all the mixture together. Like a retiree from Florida.

"What did you run in there for? I was standing right in front."

"I had to go to the bathroom."

"You didn't see me? I was right there."

Mark looked over to the spot where his father was pointing, and said, "No. I just saw the Men's room sign and went straight for it."

"Oh, OK. Well, give me a hug."

Mark walked over to his father and gave his father a hug. After a few seconds they parted and walked towards the baggage claim.

"So how was the flight?"

"It was alright. I just read my book and relaxed."

"Those JetBlue flights have the new TVs on them don't they? That is the real way to fly, television and movies for free."

"Most of the channels were just reruns of old programs."

"Oh, OK. So you just read the whole flight?"

"Yeah. It was nice actually. Although sitting for such a long time does get annoying."

"You can walk up and down the aisles you know."

"I know, I just didn't really feel like getting up. I stayed in the seat and finished my book."

"Hah. You just stayed there." Mark's father looked at him and gave a queer smile and put his arm around Mark and squeezed his shoulders.

Mark felt uncomfortable and wondered why his father insisted on picking him up at the airport.

As Mark entered the house with his suitcase as his sister Veronica rushed up from downstairs. He could hear her giggle as she ran up the stairs. She is thirty one years old, but still prances and giggles like a teenager. Mark always smiles when he sees his sister. The gleeful sister is a few inches shorter than Mark, and has the same face, but wears glasses and has long brown hair. His sister runs into a hug, and Mark picks her up as she laughs with glee. His mother comes from the back of the house, and also raises her arms and he embraces her with a firm hug. Mark's mother is a full head shorter than him. She is fully Italian in heritage, but has blue eyes and whiter skin. She has defined and strong Mediterranean features, but still looks very womanly for her age.
"How was the flight?"
"It was fine. I just read," Mark said with a shrug.
Veronica giggled again and hugged him. Mark couldn't help but laugh a little. He picked up his suitcase and moved it into his old room. There had been little changes since he moved out of the house. The bed was moved away from the window, the armoire was filled with pictures spanning time of the whole family and the desk had been moved out and a nightstand was put in its place. The wooden chair that used to accompany his desk was moved into the corner of the room.
Mark put his bag down and sat on the bed. He looked around the room and remembered what it had been like when he had lived in it. He remembered how it used to be covered in pink wallpaper after he took it over from his sister. He took off his shoes and felt that the carpet was new. It was springy and a lighter shade of white. The ceiling still had the same popcorn acoustical covering that was popular in the seventies. The walls also had a new coat of paint on them. There weren't any blemishes or dark marks from years of occupancy.
Looking around he wondered about how the week was going to be.

Walking downstairs to the lower level Mark heard the TV on and as he turned right into a hallway that extends to a family room he saw his father in a large brown La-Z-Boy™ chair. He walked towards the family room and saw his father look down the hall and give a big smile.
"Hey Mark, how's it going?"
"Not bad. Just relaxing a bit."
The downstairs room was very cold. Mark wondered why his parent's didn't keep the heat up at a higher temperature. His father had a blanket on his legs and was wearing sweats with a hood.
As long as Mark could remember, his parents insisted on keeping the house at a

reasonable temperature during the winter. The heater would not be on for longer than it had to be and everyone was encouraged to wear a sweater and socks. Mark could remember defiantly wearing shorts into January, but spending large amounts of time in his room next to the heater.

"What do you want to watch?'"

Mark thought about TV programs for a second while sitting down on the couch. He liked MacGyver, Animaniacs, sometimes the A-Team.

"I don't really watch that much TV Dad. I don't really have time. After work and the gym I usually just read until I fall asleep."

"Oh, well what have you been reading?"

"I just finished a book last week about medieval Scythian tombs that were uncovered in the steppes of Russia." As Mark said this he knew that it would be a conversation stopper.

"Oh. Tombs in Russia. Sounds interesting."

His father huddled deeper into the blanket and looked back at the TV. Mark turned his face at the TV as well and spent the next hour watching a program involving a pretty girl being abducted by terrorists, who turned out to be a politician's daughter, so the terrorists could plant a bomb in the building where the politician worked. Mark was bored.

Mark's old room was part of the hallway leading from the kitchen to the master bedroom. The door to Mark's room shuddered whenever somebody walked by it. In the early morning when his mother and father would get up and walk through the house it would rock and jitter and wake Mark up. After the first two times Mark stuffed a shirt under it so that it wouldn't move.

Walking into the field behind his house Mark saw the poppies and could smell the pine trees just a short walk away. It was that time when the sun was warm and encouraged the trees to let off their scent, but still too early for the massive amounts of yellow pollen to fill the air. Mark's chair from his room was there, and he sat down and took a harmonica out of his pocket. He always felt that it was a tad ironic that he played the harmonica, seeing as how his last name was Harmon.

Pushing and pulling the air in and out of the little groove machine he played five notes repetitively until he found a rhythm that he liked. Tapping his foot on the grass and hearing the crunch underneath his toes he started to play. He imagined a bass and drum filling in the holes between the rhythm, and he kept the time with them in his head.

Mark looked around as he took a break and heard the swish of the long dry grass. He looked down the field and saw a young doe. It went behind a bush and then changed into a short pretty girl with brown hair around her shoulders. From behind the bush he could see the outline of her shoulders and hips. The girl was short, but not too short. She had a beautiful body, there was something familiar about it.

Mark's door opened to his room.

"What are you still doing in bed? Come on, we got things to do today."

Mark's father walked through his room and opened the blackout shade to let in the light from outside. At the moment, Mark could think of something worse than his alarm clock.

"Come on. I got a job up at the Devon's house. You want to come and help me prep the house for painting?"

Mark looked up bleary eyed at his father. "No, I'm good."

"You don't want to help your father with the job?"

"No."

As Mark's eyes started to clear and he saw his father standing at the foot of his bed looking down at him, looking into his face to see if he was playing a game or trying to be funny. Mark was not.

"Um, alright then. I will go alone."

He walked out of the room and headed to the garage to pack up his materials for the day.

Mark turned over and wondered what he would do to start the day.

Walking into the kitchen he fixed himself a bowl of granola and a glass of tea. He walked downstairs to the TV room and flipped through the channels. The TV package that his family had bought came with three hundred channels. He was confident he could find something.

After ten minutes he came to an all men's TV channel network. They had on a rerun of MacGyver. Mark nestled into the chair and drank his tea.

Veronica poked her head around from an anteroom adjacent to the TV room and said, "Mornin' Giuseppie." When much younger Mark had an obsession with his Italian heritage. During this phase his sister gave him the nickname of Giuseppie, being as how Joseph was his middle name and Giuseppie is the Italian equivalent.

"Mornin' V. Whatcha up to?"

"Just doing some editing on this chapter. I am going to send it next week, and hopefully my advisor will actually read it and get it back to me in time."

Veronica was living at home because she needed a place to finish her dissertation. She is finishing a PhD in Linguistics at University of California Davis. She completed all her credits at the UC for her coursework as well as all the available semesters she could teach with her teacher's aide status. Coming back home enabled her free room and board to be able to finish the last requirement for her degree. It had been a long and hard process which was only complicated more so by university politics and lack of punctual timing.

She had been home for six months and was not much further in her dissertation than when she had left Texas. Her mother and father didn't understand what was taking her so long. She had all the time in the world to work and seemed to be working, but was not completing anything. They didn't understand why she couldn't just finish the work and turn it in. She had outlines and books and research already prepared for the book. Also, she had the Stanford library only twenty minutes away if she needed more books.

The lack of results in the time she had been home was aggravating to her parents, but at the same time they felt they had no real way to be critical. Sharon and Todd Harmon did not go to college. They had taken different paths after completing high school. While working and starting a family on the peninsula near San Francisco they saw the need and importance of having an education in order to get a job. From the time the children were able to start school they absolutely required them all to go to college. Each school year was a reminder that the kids would go to college, and if they worked hard early on, they could go to a good college and do well.

When Veronica was out of classes to take and time to teach they offered their downstairs bedroom and anteroom for her to finish her dissertation. A few years previously it had been occupied by Sharon's mother, but she had passed away and since then it had been converted into a TV room.

It seemed an easy fix to Veronica's problem, and they enjoyed the idea of having their daughter back home for a while. Sharon liked the idea of having someone in the house other than Todd, and Todd liked that his daughter was home so he could have someone to talk to about 'intellectual things.'

"How is it coming?" Mark hates to ask this question, but it comes out before he could censor it. In his mind he knows that he does not understand what it takes to actually formulate a dissertation; an original idea. He thinks about the stories he has heard of academics doing hours of research and painstaking labor and writing a chapter and editing and turning it in only to have your advisor reject it on a number of reasons. Then correcting it and resubmitting only to have the advisor reject it only for the reason that the previous ideas that they said should have been omitted, were now necessary to the chapter.

After Mark was finished with college he came to the conclusion that academics lived their lives for two reasons. One was to ensure the sadistic tradition of being an advisor to a pupil, and inflicting the same pain and stress on the student as they had received while they were studying in college. The other was to write articles, papers or books that would then be read by very few other academics and at a yearly conference they would present their ideas to their colleges and all would share in momentary fame in an intellectual circle jerk.

"It's alright. I think that I will be able to complete the chapter this weekend even

though there will be a lot of distractions around."
"Cool. Let me know if there is anything I can do."
"You watchin' MacGyver?"
"Of course, what else?"
"Some things never change." She shakes her head and heads back into her room.

Mark puts on his running shoes and heads up the drive way. He starts running through his old neighborhood. Up hills and down into the main roads that connect distant suburban communities.

He comes to a reservoir and runs along side it inhaling the dusty air and trying to push his legs further. He looks into the distance and sees a hill a few miles away, and just flat land until them. He is lost by the complete vastness of it all. His run descends into a jog, and he feels his body ache at the idea of getting to the hills so far away. He pushes the feeling down deeper into his stomach and runs as fast and hard as he can. He runs until his knees hurt, until his ankles feel like they are hinges about to become undone, until his head can't point any further. He runs hard and fast and gulps air like he is drowning.

Now seated by the reservoir, he feels drained. His legs are like lead weights and he can't think except that he knows he should just sit and look at the water for a while.

Mark looks back in the distance and sees the hill where his parents' house is. The house looks so small and he feels like he can grab it from this far away. He thinks about the buildings on the day after Tom died. How much they seemed like props for everything. He could see the other communities and they had the same falseness to them. He wondered why he had come back for Christmas. It didn't make much sense to him at the moment. He would have been much happier in Boston, even it if was freezing cold and there was little to do except read and rent movies.

He wanted to run a marathon in that moment. He wanted to run as hard and long as he could. Standing up and hitting the dust off himself he started back home at a trot.

Mark walked back into the house and went to his room. After showering and getting dressed he went to the kitchen. The door to the garage opened up as he was drinking a glass of water.

"Hey, I am headed off to Home Depot to buy some supplies for tomorrow. Want to come along?"

Mark thought about the morning and felt like he should accompany his father. If he did not spend some time with him, he felt that the vacation was going to be harder.

"Yeah, sure. Let me finish this water."

"OK, I will wait in the truck."

Mark headed up to the truck and sat in the passenger seat. His father had on the local smooth jazz station. It was playing a mixture of synthesized guitar and piano with a synthesized saxophone. Mark remembered the music from his childhood when he and his brother and sister had to help their father in the garden on the weekends. In the spring it was weeding and cutting grass in the back field. Summer was pruning the big cypress trees and making sure the ground cover was cultivated and watered so that it didn't dry out. Autumn was picking up pine needles and cutting out the parts of the plants that had succumbed to the heat of the summer. All throughout the time there had always been the smooth jazz. Early in Mark's childhood he had associated certain types of music with uncomfortable or unhappy things. The Smooth Jazz station was one. Another was Neil Diamond. Whenever Mark heard the song Sweet Caroline or Coming to America, it brought out a feeling of needing to vomit and head butt a wall at the same time.

"I need to get some gas real quick on the way."

"No problem."

"So, how's Boston?"

"It's fine. Cold right now. There isn't much going on except the normal holiday stuff."

"Did you have a Christmas with your roommates?"

"Yeah, we had a small one. It was more of a dinner though. They all had a test last week, so they really had to spend more time paying attention to that."

"Did you get anything from the people at work?"

"There was the normal gifts and stuff. Got and gave some cards."

His father looked over at him while driving to scrutinize his face and then looked back to the road.

"Did that man you saved give you anything?"

"I got a bottle of wine and a card about a week after from his family."

"You got nothing for Christmas? That seems odd. I thought you would have gotten money or a gift or something."

"Nah, I think he left early for Christmas to go be with his grandchildren in New York."

"Hmm, OK. Well, how is everything at work?"

Mark wondered if he should explain about Tom. It had happened very recently so it had not come up in conversation with the calls home.

"Actually not so good. The guy that I replaced at the office passed away a few weeks ago."

"Oh, that's sad. Was it something serious?"

"Well, it was something different. It happened when we were at the gym."

"You were there?"
"Yeah. I was a few feet from him, and after he collapsed I tried to help him a bit but there were a few doctors working out at the same gym and they took over. He passed away while en route to the hospital."
"So you were there for the whole thing, while he collapsed and then died in the hospital?"
"Yeah."
His father turned his mouth to the side and furrowed an eyebrow.
"It just seems that you have some bad luck."
"Tell me about it."

Driving off the on ramp they came up to an intersection with gas stations on opposing corners. The one nearer was a cent cheaper then the one across the street.
Todd pulled at the steering wheel and angled it towards the nearer one, although it was two lanes of traffic away. With the honking of other cars surrounding the car they made their way to the station. Mark could see yellow caution tape surrounding the gas pumps and said, "I think that they might be closed Dad."
Pulling up along side one Todd said, "The control panel is still on. I think that means they are still in service."
"But there is caution tape around the whole thing."
"Let's just see if it will give us service."
Todd slide his card through the slot and the control panel came to life. He unscrewed the cap to his gas tank and started to fill up.
A lady from inside the store started to walk out. She was a squat Mexican woman with a big smile on her face.
She came over to the machine and nodded to Todd.
"Sorry sir, but the machines are closed down."
"But the control panel is still on. If they are closed down then why didn't you turn them off."
"Oh, sorry about that, but the caution tape was supposed to let people know that the machines are off."
"The machines aren't off, I am pumping gas right now."
"OK sir. But please, the caution tape is supposed to let you know that the machines are to be off."
"I know what they mean, I can read. Fine then, I will go to another station," Todd said with a huff, and pulled the gas hose from his tank. After waiting a second he took his receipt from the machine and started the car. Once Todd had closed the door he had muttered the word 'Mexican' under his breath. The woman had a smile on her face as they drove off.
They drove in silence to Home Depot.

Entering the anteroom that is now Veronica's workroom, Mark sensed the cozy little home Veronica had made for while she worked. The TV was on, and the background noise of the basketball game is what kept Veronica company while she worked.

"Hey Giuseppie. Whatcha up to?"

"Nothing. I was just reading, and decided to take a break. What are you up to?"

"I am just editing this chapter and trying to think of a different way to change this thing here."

Mark walked over to the bookshelf behind her and perused the shelf of the family library. It occurred to him that the shelves contained some books from authors that he liked. Mark Twain, John Steinbeck and even some historical fiction. There was a sparse but effective collection of classics in this little room. The editions of the books were all twenty or thirty years old, and the binding still looked to be in good shape.

Extending his hand up to the book shelf, he used his finger to select a book. It moved over the shelf swaying back and forth as if it there was a homing beacon hidden in one of the books. His finger finally came upon Mark Twain's, <u>Roughing It</u>. Mark tipped the book on the shelf from the tip of the spine. It came willingly into his hands, and when he had finally cradled it in his palms, he noticed that the spine had a very thick layer of dust. He used his hands to wipe off the dust. After he looked up at the shelf, and ran his finger on the spines of the others on the shelf. They all had a thick layer of dust. There was also a thick layer on the base of the shelf.

He wiped his hand on his jeans, but still saw the dark shades on his fingertips from the years of dust. Looking up at the shelf, he knew that the books had not been touched in years.

Mark muttered in a low tone, "Why have a library if you aren't going to read the books. What good does it do?"

Veronica swiveled around in her chair, and said, "What was that Giuseppie?"

"Oh, nothing, I was just looking at the collection here."

Christmas morning came. Mark woke up at seven, and felt the excitement of presents. He remembered running out of bed early in the morning when he was younger and running around the house so his parents would get up.

He smiled at the thought, and turned over and went back to sleep. Eventually he heard his sister run up the stairs and start to wake everyone up. Her giggling was infectious, and Mark found himself with a contact high from her state of delirium.

They waited to open presents once Matt, Mark's brother, had come over from San Jose as they had done in the past. Presents were given out to the person, then everyone dove right in and tore them apart, then everyone said what they got for Christmas.

Brunch was afterwards, and then everyone went about their business.

In the afternoon Mark started watching a movie that he had been given.

He heard the footsteps of his father halfway through the movie, and saw his father lumbering towards the TV room. Mark smiled and moved out of the La-Z-Boy™ when he saw his father coming.

"Oh, no, don't worry about that, sit in the chair."

"No, it's OK, it is your chair."

"Yeah, but you were there first."

"It's alright Dad."

They watched the movie together. After a few minutes Todd moved uncomfortably in his chair. The movie was not to his liking.

"Do you mind if we change the channel to something else?" Todd says glumly.

"It is actually a movie, but if you want to watch something else that's fine."

"Oh, well if it is a movie, then…"

"No Dad, it is fine." Mark took the remotes and turned the movie off and set it to the cable network.

The channel came on to a TV detective series that Todd watched normally in the evening.

"Oh, I have seen this one, but it is a good one."

Mark did a mental nod and looked at the TV. He mentally set five minutes before he could politely excuse himself and go and read one of the books that he got as presents.

At the next commercial break, Mark sensed he could make a getaway from the television and started to move when his father began to speak.

"You know, there is something I wanted to talk about with you. It is about the presents we gave you."

"OK." Mark sat thinking perplexed about what it was that was so important.

"Your mother and I gave you a lot of books for Christmas. We spent a lot of money on those books."

Mark nodded.

"I feel, and I am not alone in this feeling. There are other people who feel this way too. That what you do with the books is not something that we want."

"What is that?"

"Well, you know how you give them away after you read them. I feel, and I am not the only one, that we spent a lot of money on those books. And if you give them away then that is like we spent the money for nothing."

"Dad... I give them away because I rarely read a book a second time. I give them away to people if I think they will like it, then that is my way of keeping the book in circulation and also giving a gift that has some thought."

"But we spent money on those books. And we gave them to you."
"Right. It is a present."
"Yes, well, we feel that we would like you to send them home after you read them. That way we can keep them in the family."
Mark thought about the bookshelf in the anteroom. He thought about the dust on the shelves and about the forgotten sheaves of paper.
Mark realized his father was asking him to give back his presents.
"You want me to give them back after I am done?"
"I want you to send them back so we can keep them in the family."
Mark thought about his father's choice of words and for some reason felt pity.
"Yeah Dad, fine."
Mark turned his head and effectively stopped the conversation. His father watched in silence. After a few minutes Mark got up and went to his room. He picked up one of his books and started to read it. While reading, Mark felt like the story had a bitter taste. He stopped and put it down; the book only had a short life to live.

The family always had dinner together without fail every night. It was something that both parents insisted on and the kids fell in tow with the custom. Mark and Veronica sat next to each other and across from their mom. Todd sat at the head of the table. Coming through the dining room, he put his glass that had previously held two different helpings of scotch in the dishwasher and poured himself a new glass of red wine.
Looking at the glass, Mark saw the discussion of tonight's dinner would most likely be dominated by his father. When Todd drank, which was every night, he felt the need to express himself at his dinner table.

"How is Boston sweetie? Is the job alright for you?" Sharon asked Mark.
Mark always enjoyed talking to his mom about things in Boston. She was curious about the city and the people. Sharon had expressed her sadness at not visiting more cities. She had grown up in San Francisco, and had not traveled much outside of it.
"Boston is cold. It is starting to get into the bad part of winter where it doesn't matter how much clothing you wear, you are just plain cold."
"Well, you're the one who chose to go there," She said with a furrowed brow.
"Yeah, I know. It has been a good experience so far. I can say for certain though that I am not going to live on the east coast forever. It is just not the same as California."
"I bet that is right. Here we got food and people who actually talk to one another. Open minded people and good schools," Todd chimed in.

"Yeah, that's true," Mark turned to his mother, "I don't know what it is, but California is just more of my home. I would still like to see what else there is out there, but for now, I am content learning about New England a bit."
"How many Red Sox games have you been to?" Veronica questioned.
"Oh, a few. When there are good tickets available or when I can go. I never really enjoyed watching sports though, so it is more of an occasional thing."
Veronica had been a Boston Red Sox fan since childhood. She had loyalty for the San Francisco Giants as well, but idolized Roger Clemens as a little girl, and since then has always followed the ball club.
"I tell you though, Fenway Park is a really good stadium. It seats about thirty thousand, and every game is packed. There is a real strong following when it comes to all sports in Boston, and it is a really good time when you want to see a game."
"I have heard. I will get there eventually," Veronica said with glee.
"How are you doing with saving for your trip honey?" Sharon said.
"I am doing alright. I won't go until I have enough saved, but I think I might be able to leave within the next year or so."
"So you are going to travel instead of taking advantage of working in this financial institution?" Todd said.
"Yeah. I know that finance isn't for me, but it has been a nice education about how the system works."
"So you think you know how the system works? When you start selling and trying to advertise a product is when you know how a system works." Todd took a gulp of wine from his glass. "That is how I learned about the wine industry when I worked for Young's Market. I learned all about the wineries here in the peninsula and how it is distilled and how it is made. There wasn't one thing that I didn't study or ask about. I even visited a few wineries up in Sonoma. Your mother and I went to that one Fetzer winery and had a good time. They were doing some sales pitch, and we got to stay in a cottage on the property. It was a good time, beautiful vineyard."
Mark looked up from his plate. He had been listening, but not too closely.
"Yeah, well, I don't know everything about the finance industry, but it is nice to at least see parts of it. After a while of asking questions you find out how the paperwork is organized, and that it is never really organized, and how to buy and sell and etc."
"Of course you would do research. That is how I raised all three of you. You all ask questions and learn about where you are. It is in your nature."
"Yeah. I would rather travel though. I had a great time in Europe before Boston, and now I would like to see more places. Mexico and Central America and South America would be nice."
"Well when you get to Mexico you will be surprised with how cheap everything

is. Also, the people aren't really that civilized or organized, it will be chaos and you might have to pay some people extra to get through."

"I am not sure about that, but I am curious about what the culture is like and it will be nice to speak Spanish again. I am out of practice since teaching English in Spain, but I think it is still good enough to travel."

"Well I am sure. I read articles about the place, the kidnappings and murders and corruption. I am not sure if I would want to travel there, but do what you want."

"There is still kidnappings and murders and corruption here in the U.S. In fact you open up the newspaper and it seems like that is all there is."

"It is news about the world. If there were good things to write about they would write about it."

"Maybe."

Mark prodded the last bits of food on his plate and put it into his mouth. He hoped dinner would end soon so that he could go back to his book.

"At least we talked you out of the stupid Saudi Arabia idea."

Mark remembered when he was in Boston, still excited about having traveled in Europe and had sent resumes out to schools to teach English across the world. He had got an offer from a school in Saudi Arabia, and pondered the job possibility for a few weeks while being harangued by his family.

"Yeah. I would still like to live in the Middle East for a while. It would be a good experience."

His father guffawed. "Good experience? They are a bunch of people who don't respect life, and there are killings and genocide every day."

"Well, the Middle East is a very big place. There is a lot of people living there, and it isn't exactly a peaceful time, but most of the countries are actually quite normal. Just people who want to work and live, and do so. It would be interesting to live in a Muslim culture."

"They don't respect life; they feel like it is something that is just wasted on rats. They kill each other every day over nothing except their religion just like they're were squashing ants," Todd squashes an imaginary ant on the table with his thumb and wiggles his elbow right and left to show the force that was used.

"I know. I read the paper every day about how many people have died, and they all have guns and hate Americans."

"I don't think that's the truth. But, hopefully I will know someday. I would like to learn Arabic also. Another language and writing system would be interesting."

"They are all pretty uneducated unless they are rich. It won't be easy to live there. They will hate you or use you because you are white and American."

"I am not sure about that, but I would like to find out for myself," Mark said flatly.

Mark put his fork down on his plate and put his hand up to his mouth to cough. His mother saw that he disliked the direction of the conversation, and changed the subject to Christmas.
Soon after, dinner was done.

Mark walked into the room and sat on the bed. His desk chair was still in front of the window where he had left it from before.

He looked at the chair and thought about his ex-girlfriend from college. She had visited the house while they were still in school. It was during the summer when Mark was working as a handyman in the neighborhood so he could save money for tuition and the apartment. She had come for three days.

His father commented about how they were in love. Also about how she seemed quiet and nice and that he could see that she loved him very much. Mark looked at the chair and thought about the morning that his parents left to go get groceries for the week. How Danielle had been awoken in the morning by them and went into Mark's room after they left to climb into bed with him. They slept soundly together, then got up and took a shower.
When they were getting dressed they had started playing games and tricks with each other and ended up making love in the chair.
Now the chair was sitting in the sun. Light was shinning brightly on its deep stained wood. Mark stood up and picked up the chair. It was warm to his touch like skin. He moved it back into the corner out of the light. Sitting back down on his bed he looked out of the window and felt like he was crying inside his throat. His nose felt stuffy and he leaned back against the headboard of the bed. Closing his eyes, he fell asleep deeply.

Chapter 12 - Covet

Trodding through the snow, Mark purposefully aimed for undisturbed ice in the early morning.
After the flight and train, he had an hour and a half to get dressed and go to work. Walking into the apartment, he feels a sense of security and is glad to walk through the doorway. The apartment is cold from no one being inside of it for a week, and he feels glad that the whole place is to himself.
He strips off his clothes and runs into the warmth of the shower. He goes through his routine feeling slightly light-headed from the lack of sleep. With an hour to spare he leaves for work early and goes by the diner around the corner to get some breakfast.

Reaching his doorway after his first day back to work Mark heard, "Hey Mark, how was Christmas back home?"
Mark heard the voice of his downstairs neighbor through the stairwell. He walked over to the doorway, and yelled down, "It was alright. I could use another vacation though."
"Yeah, I know the feeling. Hey man, come down. I am making cookies."
"Cool. I will be down in a sec."
Mark changed his clothes and headed down. Walking down the stairs to Amalie's apartment Mark felt the cold unheated air of winter. It is fucking cold.
"Hey love, what kind you making?"
"I am doing chocolate chip and also my version of cherries and pecans."
"Sweet."
"So, tell me, how was the Christmas with the parents?"
"Eh, you know. Same shit, different year. Presents, cookies, giggling sisters, drunk fathers. It all just kind of melts together to form the holiday we all know and love."
"Sweet. Yeah I stopped in general going to any holidays with the family. It has turned out to be a better policy. This way I get to hang out without anyone for a week, and say that I need vacation with the family, when I am really just walking around my apartment in my underwear and making cookies."
"Sounds like a philosophy we all should live by. Misdirection and cookies."
Amalie smiles and dives into another batch of cookies.
"Hey can I check your internet for a sec?"
"Yeah, no prob. It is your internet anyways," Amalie says with a giggle. "I steal whoever has an open signal at the time. I am a pirate." Amalie covers her left eye and straightens her right leg as though it is a peg leg as she walks into the kitchen.

Mark furrows a brow and walks to her computer. After checking his email he logs on to the blog page that he has. His friends are listed as well on his page, and he perused one. On the page of his best friend is a comment from his ex-girlfriend, Danielle. She has a page as well, and Mark has not checked it in a while so he clicks on her name and is transported to her page. After reading some information he sees comments from her friends, old roommates, and one of the pictures of her birthday.

It happened recently, and Mark sent an email wishing a happy birthday, but did not receive a reply back. Their relationship had been long and Mark had broken up with her several times. Since Danielle, Mark had not been with anyone else, and still went to sleep thinking about her. When he was lonely she was usually his first thought, and he was usually tempted to call her, but knew that the conversation would as always be something that was unfulfilling and solely small talk. Mark knew that Danielle had feelings for him, and Danielle knew about Mark's feelings as well, but the two did not interact well outside of a relationship. Together they would dive into affection and feel the vespers of love, but apart they would become bored or annoyed that they could not talk about the things that they wanted to, which was mostly each other.

Looking at the pictures posted of her birthday party, Mark saw that there was a guy in them with her. The guy had his arm around her shoulders. Looking at the captions of the pictures, he noticed that the guy had a name, it was Scott. Further down in her profile, Mark saw that there was a section for **Relationship** and it was filled in with **IN A RELATIONSHIP**.

Mark looked again at the profile. Danielle now had a new boyfriend. He had heard about a guy that she was dating, but it was official. She put in on her page. She had pictures up of him and her together. She was with someone else.

Inside the conflicting emotions drove Mark to the couch behind him. He wasn't sure what to feel. It had been two years since they had broken up. Plenty of time, and she of course, could be with another guy if she wanted. But she hadn't before, and now she was. Mark wanted to know more, but in order to do that he would have to call Danielle and ask her questions that would show him to be some jealous ex-boyfriend. He was not quite sure that was what he wanted. Mark went back to the computer. He looked at the pictures again. The guy was tall, thin, white, and had thick brown hair parted down the middle and was wearing a black blazer. Mark did not like him. Something about him seemed like he was a used bible salesman.

Looking at one of the captions of the photos, Mark saw that it was written by one of Danielle's friends. It read, 'You and Scott are SUPER nuts for leaving in the middle of the night! The other two girls left so I had the bed ALL TO

MYSELF."

Mark thought about this caption. The meaning of leaving in the middle of the night. Scott and Danielle together. Leaving early, on the night of a party. Drunk, happy, tipsy. They went back to her place so they could have sex. Mark clawed his pants at the thought of this. Mark felt slightly angered at seeing this image, but at the same time felt that it was pointless to feel this way because she was not his girlfriend anymore. Mark felt the need to drink alcohol.

"Hey Amalie, you know I am pretty tired after the flight yesterday and this week with work and all that crap. I think I am going to go upstairs and just read for a while and sleep. I am really in bad shape."

"You alright man? You sure?"

"Yeah, I think I am just going to go. Thanks though. I'll take a rain check."

In his room with a bottle of wine and a book of poems by T.S. Elliot, Mark sat on his bed, and stood up, and paced his room, and sat. The alcohol lifted his irritation. He felt happier and less aware of the fact that his ex-girlfriend was being prodded by some guy.

In the middle of reciting The Love Song of J. Alfred Prufrock, Mark stopped and felt jealousy run through his bones. He took up his phone, and decided to let out some of his feelings.

In the phone he typed the message, "I just saw a picture of him. He is wearing a fucking blazer. I want to beat his 80's mullet off his slanted head."

Mark put the phone down, and laid back. He put the bottle to his lips and drank the last of the wine. Falling into a dream, he felt cold and as though sleep was a rude intrusion on his night of poetic recitations.

In the morning Mark woke up, and felt that the light coming into his room was too bright. He saw the bottle next to his bed, and remembered what had transpired. He checked his phone, and the message had been sent, but to his friend Eric. Luckily he had not sent it to Danielle in his stupor. He laid back and fell asleep again, slightly relieved.

Mark woke up again, and felt his way to the shower. Luckily it was Saturday, and he did not need to do anything. No one was around, he was alone, and he wanted a burrito. Mark thought for a second about where he could get a burrito. He then remembered he was in Boston, and there was not a decent Mexican restaurant. There were no Mexicans around, they preferred warmer climates. Mark thought about what would possess anybody to live in an area that turns frigidly cold. Didn't cavemen learn to go south in the winter, or maybe that was ducks?

Mark thought about what to do for the day. He was still upset from the discovery of 'The Prodder." Looking outside, Mark knew it was going to be cold. He felt the need to refresh his belief, so he stuck his hand outside. It was so cold that as soon as he opened up the window, he felt goose pimples on his scrotum.

After feeling sufficiently chilled, Mark closed the window. He thought about renting some movies, and maybe getting some Chinese food.

He put on his clothes and walked to the video store. He walked through the aisle of the independent movie store, and found what he was looking for. A section dedicated solely to Kung Fu and Hong Kong action. He picked out five movies that involved fighting, swords, samurai, blood, gore, and the minute possibility of love for the main character.

Walking to the counter with the movies in his hands, they all felt like little boxes containing happiness tantamount to Belgian chocolates or a hefty inhalation from a bong.

Mark walked back to his apartment feeling as though he had been saved and given the chance to be forgetful. He gladly walked into the door, and up to his apartment, thinking about the fight scenes and carnage he was about to view. He tore off his outer shell, and thrust a movie into the player. Sitting on his couch he put a blanket over himself, and waited for the blood to start.

His phone started to ring at the moment of the beginning credits. It was his friend Eric.

"Hey, Eric. What's up?"

"Hey, what's going down my man?"

"Not much, just chillin' watching some movies."

"Cool. So…I got your text message last night."

"Ah, yeah. That. Uh, well, it seems that I saw a picture of Danielle's boyfriend on Myspace, and proceeded to get drunk and then I wrote you a message."

"Really. Yeah. Man, that message was pure hate. I was so taken back by it."

"Yeah, I know, I guess that I could have done something a little better, but that just came out."

"Ah. Did you write one to Danielle?"

"I don't think so. I hope not. I can't imagine what I would have written to her."

"Yeah. It would be interesting."

"I can't believe that I went on a binge like that. It has been two years since we broke up. I mean, I shouldn't be feeling anything like that for her. It was weird."

"Dude, you guys were together for three years. You are going to feel something when she ends up with another guy."

"I know, you are right, but still, you know, it is just weird. I mean the reaction was pretty violent. I don't normally get drunk and send out hate messages."

"Yeah, well, at least you know you still have feelings. It is better than being in denial and saying that it is all over with."

"I guess. It would still be nice if it didn't piss me off."

"Yeah, well, that is what happens when you break up with a girl. You get pissed off when she is with someone else."

"I hate to feel all human, but yeah, it pisses me off. What can you do?"

"What can you do?"

Mark shifted in his seat and put down his plate of Chinese food.

"Alright man, I am off to go hike with Anika."

"Yeah, cool, thanks for the call. I appreciate it."

"No problem. Peace."

"Later bro."

Chapter 13 - Purpose

Walking past the bullpen, Mark looked over at Ly. Looking at the Vietnamese girl, Mark saw certain features about her face that reminded him of Danielle. In fact, Ly was the same height, had the same type of face, and even acted very similar. Mark shrugged it off as something as simple as the two being of Asian ancestry, but looking back at Ly he felt nervous. Now he had a reminder of Danielle at the office. This did not make him happy.

Mark is sitting at his desk considering whether or not to check the Yahoo! News website. If he views it this early in the day he will be deprived of the mediocre pleasure later when there is sure to be a rather long lull in the day.
His phone lights up and he sees that Paul is calling him.
"Hey Paul."
"Hey Mark, How's it going?"
"Not bad. What's up?"
"You know, my machine is acting up. I am trying to move the mouse and it won't move at all."
"Really. Did you nudge the machine at all this morning? Or maybe wiggle any wires?"
"Well, last night before I left I replaced the mouse with one from home. Could that have done anything?"
I wonder, thinks Mark.
"I bet that is what caused it. All you need to do is turn the machine off and back on."
"Turn it off. OK. That sounds easy. Which button is that on? On the front or back?"
There are not any buttons on the back of the machine. Conversations like this one make Mark feel dispirited, and his shoulders start to droop.
"Don't worry Paul, I will be right over there."
Mark isn't sure if he should run-walk to Paul's office to complete the monotonous task of showing Paul where the power button is on the front of the machine, labeled appropriately with 'POWER,' or if he should slowly walk so he can secretly show his contempt as well as use up more time during the day so it will not be quite as long.
"Hey Paul."
"Morning Mark," Paul replied gladly.
Mark walked over to the machine and pressed the power button until he heard the machine turn off. Then he pressed it again so the power went back on.
"This should take care of it." Mark stated unemotionally.

"I will stick around just for a sec to make sure it is working."
Once the windows sign showed up Mark moved the mouse, and it responded on the screen with the little white pointer moving appropriately.
'"Wow Mark, you fix everything around here."
Anything with a plug, Mark thought joylessly.

Chapter 14 - Fly on a wall

Mark walked to the bullpen to a computer station that was on his list to fix. He stared at the screen typing in the robotic commands when he noticed Noelle swivel around in her chair from across the row.
"Hey guys. I am hungry, what should I get for lunch?" Noelle says to the open bullpen.
"Why don't you go and get a hamburger or a deli sandwich," Geno says helpfully.
"Nah, go and get some sushi, that is the best," says Ly.
Paul Rose was walking by and pipes up, "You know sushi is supposed to be the best for you. Raw vegetables and no grease. The Asian foods are supposed to be the better way to go."
"I don't know, I have never been a big fan of Asian food."
"No, Asian is the best you can get. You don't want any of that grease or fried food," Ly says resolutely.
"Yeah but Asian people are so much smaller and more athletic and used to eating that way. I mean I am used to eating more than that." Noelle whimpers.
"Yeah, but Asian people are smaller because they eat that way, and healthier. If you start eating rice and fish you will be the most healthy you can be," Ly says reassuringly.
Paul chimes, "I know a place that sells good rice and teriyaki bowls. They are the best around here. Don't worry they give you enough to eat." Phil pats lightly on his paunch belly. "And about Asian food being healthier, it is the most healthy you can eat. I have lost five pounds since I started eating Asian food for lunch."
Paul neglected to mention that he started two years ago.
"Well, OK, maybe you guys are right. I can try something new for a little while. I do want to lose weight, and if it is healthy then that is alright," Noelle says reluctantly.
"Believe me Noelle, I am Vietnamese, and I know that the food is healthy. The way that Asian people live is so much better than the way westerners live. It is meant more for you to live with nature, and not against it," Ly says definitively.
"OK," Noelle says standing up. "I will try that teriyaki place out."
Mark clicked away at the computer, feeling a pain in his stomach from the superlatives and generalized statements that had just saturated the room.

Chapter 15 - Sex Appeal

Looking ahead at the brokers in the office ten feet away, Noelle opened up her desk drawer stealthily so no one could see what she was taking out. After dipping her hand into the drawer, she pulled out a yellow box of girl scout cookies. It was two months after the girl scouts had stopped selling them, and she knew that if anyone saw the cookies, she would not be able to say no to them. However, the idea of keeping the cookies all to herself was exciting. If she could hold them in her lap, and sneak a couple of cookies out of the box, the stealth and secrecy would make her feel truly invisible. She put the cookies on her lap and tucked her legs under her desk so that the box was as hidden as it could be. With one hand on the keyboard to feign typing, she slowly put the other hand down into the box. There were plastic wrappers from the individual packages of cookies at the entrance of the box. She felt along the entrance to find the cookies themselves. Using her fingertips as eyes, she contorted her hand to probe for the package of cookies. She tried to flex her fingers so she did not make any sound against the plastic wrappers. Finally, she found a cookie that must have fallen out of the wrapper previously. She hesitated for a moment thinking about what the effects are on a cookie in the open air without the protective plastic covering, but still inside the box. She decided to go ahead and eat the cookie anyway.

She pinched the cookie in between her index finger and middle finger and drew the cookie out of the cardboard box slowly. She was careful not to make a noise.

She realizes her right hand has been still and starts to hit the keyboard to make it look like she is working.

She brings her left hand to her mouth while faking a cough. Just before she pulls her hand away she puts a cookie in her mouth.

She hits the crumbs off her hand on the side of her skirt and savors in the cookies' chocolate and caramel delight.

Geno was watching Noelle throughout the entire episode with the cookie. At first, he was curious about why Noelle would put a box of cookies on her lap, and then he just focused on her round and plump rear end.

In his mind he was pinching it and squeezing it while she fawned over him and rubbed her chest and hips against him.

Sitting at his desk, Mark was going through his files to see that everything was alphabetized and in order.

The phone started ringing and Mark saw it was Joanne. He thanked god that

there was an excuse to put the files down.
"Hey Joanne."
"Hey Mark. I have some files here that I need to be stored in another room. When you have a chance can you get Vinny's hand truck and move them?"
"Yeah, no problem. I will be right up."
Mark got the hand truck and headed up to the twenty-eighth floor.
There was a stack of twelve boxes in her office stacked neatly in rows of three.
"Here they are. Go ahead and put them in that room there. I went ahead and cleaned off the dust too."
Mark walked over to the room which was across the hall.
"I would do it, but my back has been giving me problems again."
"No problem," said Mark. "I didn't know that you were the maid too."
"Only on Friday nights with Rick," Joanne said with a smile.
Mark dwelt on the comment for a second in his head, and then realized Rick was her boyfriend.
Joanne had taken up her clipboard and was headed to somewhere else in the office. Mark briefly saw the image of Joanne in a short cut French maid's outfit with a feather duster in her hand. The outfit made a swishing sound as she walked away.

Putting the last stack of boxes in the room, Mark started guiding the hand truck through the hallways and towards the elevator.
Along the way he past the photocopy room and heard the motherly Trish talking inside the room. As Mark past by the room he saw Peter bending down to put paper in the machine, and as he did Trish said, "Whoa baby, would you look at that." Peter, bent over, smiled up at Trish.
Mark walked on. He came to the elevator and pushed the button. As he stepped inside two people were rounding the corner. It was Tami Stearns, a young cute blonde brokers assistant and Justin who works next to her. Mark held the elevator for them.
"Hey Mark," Tami said with a cheery voice.
"What up guy," Justin said in a tough guy Boston accent.
"Hey guys. Coffee break?"
"Yeah," Tami said nonchalantly.
"So, anyways. I found the secret when you go on a date. Do fifty pushups and a hundred sit ups before you meet the girl and then accidentally bump into her so that she feels you. It works every time," Justin sputters out to Tami.
Taking his bicep in her hand, "Oh, Justin. You are so strong, my my." She laughs as she throws away the arm.
The elevator opens up a floor down, and Mark walks into the lobby.
"Later gang," Mark says to the two.

"Bye," they say in unison.

Mark walks into the hallway towards the mailroom. He contemplates the amount of innuendo that he has just seen and heard. As he goes around the corner and into the mailroom he puts the hand truck in its original position.

"Thanks Vinny."

"Yeah, any time Mark," Vinny calls back in his thick Boston accent.

Mark looks down at the floor and tries not to think sexual thoughts. Going back into the hallway he goes past Evaline Amor. She is a pretty woman of Portuguese descent. He looks up, and sees her suit pants and violet silk blouse. Through the blouse her nipples stand erect. Forcing his eyes to match hers, he says hello.

Now feeling like he has no control over his mind, Mark walks down the hallway in slight paranoia. He turns and walks in the opposite direction wanting to take a longer walk towards his desk so that he can work the idea out of his head. He looks down at the carpet, and then looks up and sees someone coming out of operations. It is Beth, although she is wearing a bikini that is lined by white flowers and a headdress of white feathers. Her soft milky skin and blonde hair seem luxuriant, and her blue eyes shine in contrast.

Mark closes his eyes and reopens them, and sees Beth in her normal clothes and she is looking at him strangely.

"Mark, are you alright?"

Mark puts his hand up to his head and says, "I think I am very tired. I just had a weird day dream."

"I guess. You look lost. Go get some water or coffee or something."

"Yeah, good idea."

Mark wandered into the break room and sat down. He looked up at CSPAN and found comfort in the lack of sexual images in the news report about biotechnology firms on the rise.

Chapter 16 - Daily Escape

Trudging into the doorway, Richard walked into the twenty-seventh floor looking slightly like a commercial fisherman. He was wearing a long rain slick that went down to his shins. Buttoned up and with the hood on he looked like a grim reaper in a shade of blue.
Coming into the reception and hallway he unbuttoned his coat and headed for his office. While making his way through the door Nancy looked up from the reception desk and smiled.
"Hey Richard, a little cold out there?"
Richard nodded and gave a mild grunt to Nancy. Watching him walk by Nancy wondered why Richard hated her. Nancy was a lady in her late thirties and from Ohio. She wore Polartec fleece pants and a blouse to work that gave her the look of someone going to a bourgeoisie pajama party. She has a ring in her right eyebrow, and makes it a point to be nice to everyone through the door. When she can she tries to explain to everyone who will listen as to the amount of work she does and has to deal with. She is the main switchboard operator for the office, as well as the assistant for a broker. She makes more money than any brokers' assistant, but still feels that she does too much and does not know how to get anyone to help her with her workload. She is certain that every one of the managers dislikes her, and this intimidates her into thinking that she can't ask them for help.
She tries to be helpful and cheerful to everyone in the office, but usually nice and friendly is met with a cold or superficial disposition by most people in the office.
When everyone flocks to the free luncheons or goes for the leftovers after a business meeting she always asks the people who walk by to bring her back something, but few remember.
Nancy is usually forgotten by most people or is put in the back of their mind as that hello or goodbye as they leave.
It was coming close to Nancy's break and she thought about calling Maria. She wanted a few extra minutes so that she could do some things around the office.
"Hey Maria, how are ya?"
"Hey Nancy, not bad."
"Do you mind staying for a few extra minutes? I would like to go to the mail room too so that I can check for mail and also any packages."
"Yeah sure Nancy. I will be there in a few minutes."
Nancy got out her insulated lunch bag and a bottle of water and placed them neatly on the side of her keyboard. She reorganized all her stacks of paper so she wouldn't lose her place and stepped over to the fern behind her to water it.

Maria came around the corner with a magazine and smiles as she plopped in the chair.

"OK, I will be back at one o'clock."

Nancy went to the break room on the twenty-seventh floor to eat her lunch. It was small and cramped, but she preferred it because she knew more people on the twenty-seventh floor, so if they came by she could say hello. The TV inside the break room was always tuned into CSPAN, and she was not sure if she was allowed to change the channel, so she watched reports about the daily market in silence. After her lunch she walked to the mailroom and checked her box. There was nothing for her, but in her brokers' box there were letters. Some were checks, and some were IRA forms. She sifted through the daily packages and found none for her or her broker. She said hello to Vinny, and then went to operations where she put through her transfers and other chores. After operations she walked through the halls, and saw that a lunch meeting had just occurred. She sifted through the leftovers and found half a roast beef sandwich and a brownie. She pondered whether to eat in the green room, or bring it back to her desk and save it for a snack, or part of dinner. She decided to bring it back to her desk. On the way back to her desk she went to the ladies room, and then made her way to the break room again to make some tea before she went back. She contemplated making some for Maria also, and decided to bring her a fresh cup of coffee.

Walking up to the desk, she had the insulated lunch bag stuffed under an arm and two cups of hot beverage in her hands.

"Hey Maria. Thanks for giving me a few extra minutes. I appreciate it."

"Any time Nancy."

"When I made my tea, I made a cup of coffee for you too. I wasn't sure what you liked, so I just did French Roast."

"Oh, hey thanks Nancy, I appreciate it." Maria took the cup affectionately. "There was only one message for you, it was William. He said he won't be in for the rest of the afternoon."

"Oh geez, that's great. I guess I am stuck just taking messages now. Oh well, thanks."

Nancy sat back down in her chair and took some papers from the stack. Looking up she saw the sun glinting off the side of another building. She smiled to herself, and put her nose back into the papers that had to be filled out.

Larry looked down at his paperwork to be filed. There was a mountain of signatures to be done, and all he wanted was to leave and get a drink.

He looked over at his assistant Sofia, and thought about having her do the signatures. He wondered if she would do it. He had asked her in the past when he was in a rush, and she obliged with a laconic nod, but he was unsure if she would do it again.

Looking at Sofia, he was glad that he had her as an assistant. He had had a problem with the last girl that worked for him, and didn't want to repeat it. The last girl was a young, pretty and smart Asian girl right out of college. When he was bored or tired during the day he would tease and flirt with her. After a year they were sleeping together, and he only saw problems in the near future. Eventually his wife started to become aware of another perfume, more nights of Larry 'drinking' with clients, and other little personality quirks that changed about him when he was around her.

To Larry's surprise his wife didn't seem to mind the other lover, and in fact made jokes about it occasionally. Larry became nervous from his wife's lack of care. He was paranoid about her divorcing him or about his family finding out. After a month of living on the edge of a panic attack, he decided to get rid of his assistant. Afraid of the little lover too, he found her a job in a finance consulting group and swore never to hire a pretty assistant again. If he were going to cheat on his wife, he would do it with a much more subterfuge.

Looking at Sofia, he was proud of the choice he had made six years ago. She had not changed much since when he hired her. She was still a medium height black woman that was overweight after two kids and no husband, had an acne ridden face and a slight Caribbean accent from her Jamaican parents.

Her complete lack of attractiveness allowed him to be able to concentrate more on his work, and not think about sex at all. The only downside was that along with her physical deficiencies she had mental ones as well. She worked only part time, and even when she did work she would do very little. The files would be out of order, papers would not be brought to where they needed to go, and her way of speaking on the phone made her seem uneducated and slightly retarded. She would slur words and occasionally use impolite slang, when Larry knew that most of his clients were white affluent families.

Larry considered her background in the black neighborhood as her downfall, but having her in the office was more valuable to his productivity than someone who was smart and pretty. Looking at the stack of paper, Larry decided to leave them until tomorrow, picked up his coast and started for the door.

"I am off Sofia. See you tomorrow."

Larry heard a noise that sounded like a whiny 'Bye,' but he thought that there was an L in the word.

He shrugged it off, and walked to the elevator.

Chapter 17 - Civilized

In the year 1973, Goldman Saks hired a young finance consultant that it had worked with for two years from an outside group. The kid was two years out of Boston College and already the director of a team of eight consultants specializing in analysis of market trends. Goldman hired him because during an interview he had expressed an interest in selling. He understood that he could make a greater profit doing that than in consulting.

When he started at Goldman they had problems with Jon Cutter for the first two years. It wasn't that he was unaware of the market conditions, for recognizing the patterns and trends was what he loved to do most. They had problems placing him in a situation where he could thrive. They started him in wealth management, and he could not connect well with customers that were seeking to open small IRA's. They tried to put him in retail bond market, but he found selling giant amounts of bonds to corporations uninteresting. The bond market had its own trends, but he was interested more in securities and the private market of businesses. It was faster paced and required a more intimate knowledge.

Jon was a young man with a big ego, due to his confidence in knowing the market. He had a tall haircut that flopped to one side of his head and his giant thick glasses made his blue eyes look like saucers. When he spoke, he would spew out commands and rhetorical questions and then cut people off in the middle of a response so he could watch the price activity of a stock.

In general, he had little control over his emotions and contempt for anyone who would obstruct his path in trying to make money or find research. The administration of the office was always in the path of his tantrums and his cathartic escapades. Normally he was avoided, and when he started to make calls and make noise people just did what he wanted to shut him up. His personality was as an attention getter, and few people in the office found it easy to work with him. When he wasn't bullying people to see his viewpoint he acted in a very high society manner. He spoke about modern art, operas, theaters and any number of things that he felt were of a finer taste. Most people didn't understand or care to try.

Goldman eventually found a place for the young talent. Seeing as how he was difficult to deal with and had talent, but little ability to sell, they found a team in the wealth management section to take him on. It was a team with two brokers. Both were good looking men with charm and patience. One was older, and about ten years away from retirement, the other was young and had a good future ahead of him. Jon came into the group as a loud and fast-paced kid. The two brokers had seen this young talent in the office, and heard of his reputation.

The beginning of the relationship was stressful, but after a few months the team found a great way to work. Jon did his research and found every way possible to make money. The two other brokers carried out his ideas and did damage control as Jon would call up clients to convince them about his ideas. Steven and Ron were always there to criticize Jon's ideas or asking about his thinking. Jon always explained his ideas, and after seeing that these men were patient and useful to his future he would explain with less flamboyance, a sign from his as a professional courtesy. The group brought in clients and assets with exponential growth over the years. Ron retired and Steven and Jon had a partnership that became strong and fruitful.

They left the strong umbrella of Goldman due to conflicts with the administration over the constantly changing paperwork. After losing two large clients because of not knowing to file the right paperwork, they started looking for another firm.

They settled in Randley Financial Brokerage because the house gave them an offer of a new nice office, less hassles with paperwork, and a general new start away from old connections and old problems in Goldman Saks.

"Steven, look at gold there. I think it is going to jump another point today. See if we can get Barclay on the phone and put another order in." Jon shouted the command amidst a quiet room concentrating on their computer screens. Jon was seated beside him and looked patiently at the screen of changing numbers. After clicking the number for gold and opening a graph that shows the day's activity Steven spoke.

"I think you're right. Trish, can you get Barclay and Williamson also on the phone. I think we can help them out. They have been asking about taking more positions, here is one that will be small enough to wet their appetite."

'Trish' is Patricia Kramer. She has been an assistant in the office for thirty years. A short, stout woman, and with a constant smile on her face. She is a natural mother, and has no problems with taking anyone in the office under her wing. When Steven and Jon came to the office she was absorbed into the group because she had plenty of experience, could buy and sell securities and could be trusted to do everything they needed, and even teach them about the system they were changing to. Jon's overzealous personality was nothing to deal with for her; she had worked with much worse. When he would be loud and boisterous and try to seek attention in his own way she would shrug him off and laugh as she would at seeing a little boy playing and acting like he was a king.

"Let's see if we can get some options two points above the spread. I think it is going to rise another three, but I want a buffer."

"Alright Jon, let me get them on the phone first."

Steven stood up and stretched his back and legs. He was a tall athletic man that was slightly balding on the top of his head and had a thick brown mustache under his nose. He wore a white button down shirt and kept the top two buttons loose so you could see some chest hair flow out. In a certain way he looked like the Baywatch star Newman. He walked by another assistant Tim Kiziniuk. Tim was a young man who had spent four years in a desk job for a finance consulting firm, and picked up the job with the team in the hopes that he could learn about the way that they have constructed their business.

As Jon walks out of the office Natasha walks in. Natasha is about five feet tall, and next to Jon she is a dwarf. She is short, petite, and has a mousy kind of face. She sits down to her computer, and clicks away at unread messages.

"Jon, don't forget that we have that meeting with the Petersen's tomorrow. It is a lunch meeting at one, so we won't be getting any food that day. You need to bring something in so you won't be hungry."

Jon sneered a lip and looked back at his screen showing the prices of precious metals.

"Tim, what do you think about how gold is doing?"

Tim looked up from his screen as if brought out of a trance, and mumbled, "I, uh, gold has had a lot of activity in the past three months." Tim was trying to force his way into Jon's mindset now. He started clicking in the program and brought up a longitudinal graph of the activity of gold. "Looking like it has been on the rise slowly for the past three weeks, and today it jumped a point."

"Yeah, why did it jump a point today?" Jon queried bringing a finger to his lip.

"Well, it could have been because of the drop of petrol yesterday in the middle eastern market, or maybe because of the news that there was a mine in Africa that closed."

"Yes, that's possible."

"I think it will hit its high today or maybe tomorrow morning and then descend back to where it was two days ago in a couple of weeks."

Jon stared at his screen trying to see through the monitor. He usually posed questions out loud while he was reviewing the data in front of him. When he could remember he would form his thought into questions for Tim, so that he could train the recruit to think about why certain things happened.

"I think you're right Tim, I think you may be right." Jon clicked on his computer to be able to see his securities watch list. As he did, this Mark came into the corner office.

"Hey all," Mark said amiably. "I am here to change the toner cartridge for the printer here."

Mark had a special relationship of sorts with the group. Really, this relationship was with Jon, the rest of the group saw Mark as another worker in the office, and didn't pay too much attention to him. Jon primarily saw Mark as part of the office administration when Mark started to work there, and proceeded to order him and attempt to manipulate him for office supplies. Mark saw Jon as another annoying broker and did what he could to help him, but did not cow tow to the broker's ego or requests for equipment that Mark could not order. Jon eventually started to play games with Mark asking him about his view on the technology market and then eventually about governments or businesses. Jon never actually listened to Mark's replies or ideas, but instead was impressed that Mark gave him clear and concise answers that seemed more or less to be aware of the market and also aware of the world around him. Jon loved to play the open question game with Mark, and usually made an excuse to get something fixed or broken so he could ask the youth questions and generally amuse himself. More than not, Jon liked how when he pushed or tried to manipulate Mark, Mark usually did what was asked, but never gave Jon more attention or more favor than anybody else.

"Mark, I am glad you are here," Jon looked at the youth. "When are you going to fix my outlook screen here so that there isn't this glitch anymore?"

Putting the cartridges down Mark walked over to Jon and looked at his screen. After clicking on the screen and seeing the glitch Mark said, "I will have to call tech support and get them to remote in. It might take about an hour. Do you have a meeting today or lunch?"

"No, I will be here all day. How about next week?"

"Yeah, sure that will work. What day?"

"Any day, I am going on vacation so you can do it any time you want."

"Ah, there is the dilemma, you have to be logged in, and if you are away you can't log in."

"Well, I will call you this week and tell you when I have time."

"Cool. Where are you off to for vacation in this cold winter, Florida?"

"No, actually I am going to England."

"Wow, really? England? Why?"

"They are the most civilized people I have ever encountered."

Mark thought about the time he had traveled through England.

"I agree that they have a great ability to queue and superior table manners as a whole, but it depends on how you define civilized."

"Whenever I go there everyone has the utmost courtesy and respect. Nothing but the best is always put out for me and my wife. The museums and art houses are all staffed by the most professional and knowledgeable people, and I always feel like there is an elegant dance around me."

"Well, yeah, I can understand that. But Jon, forgive me for presuming, but you probably go to expensive hotels, restaurants and art galleries. Practically wherever you are, those are the places where the best is always provided. It is when you travel within the culture and mix with populace and see their way of life that you usually see a broader view of what the culture is like."

Jon turned around to his screen and picked up his phone, which was usually the signal to Mark that the conversation was over. Mark walked over to the printer and replaced the toner cartridges. While on his way out Jon put down the phone from his lips and said, "Don't forget about the computer glitch."

Mark turned and said, "Yeah, just give me call when you are ready," but before he could finish Jon had returned to his phone.

Chapter 18 - Looking glass

Mark walks slowly, and with a slight waddle, as he carries a computer monitor in his arms down the hall. He enters into the corner of Antonio Sciarelli and James Cotlin and looks to see if anyone's around. Suddenly popping her head up from under her desk, Sue Carrey gives Mark a smile.
"Hey Sue, what's going on?" Mark puts the monitor on Antonio's desk and starts to unplug cables going into the back of it.
"Hey Mark, how ya doing?"
Sue Carrey is a short stout woman from East Boston. She is the assistant for William Dorey, and has a permanent headache while around the Cotlin group. Their constant bickering has led her to near insanity many times, and occasionally makes her take a swig from a whiskey bottle that is hidden in her desk.
"Not bad, just taking care of Sciarelli's monitor here. I had one here that I could replace it with, so I won't have to hear him complain about this for a little while."
Mark started taking the pictures and mementos down from Antonio's monitor, and ended up with a pile of family pictures on the desk.
"Man, this guy has a lot of kids. I see four in the pictures."
"Yeah, and there is one more on the way."
"You got to be kidding."
"Nope, he let us know a month ago."
"Well, they are a good Italian catholic family. Five kids, and Antonio is only what, thirty one?"
"Yeah. They better start doing business like William Buckman or he isn't going to have a retirement after those five, or maybe more."
"I don't suppose anyone has ever actually mentioned the word vasectomy to him?" Mark said looking back at Sue.
"Actually he had one. He got it reversed last year because his wife wanted more babies. You can tell who wears the pants in that family."
Mark looked at the pretty Italian face and hour glass figure of Antonio's wife. In the picture she looks sweet and has strong shoulders. Then Mark thinks about how behind a closed bedroom door she is domineering and lecturing of her husband who pleads rationality about having another kid. She wants another, and she wants it with him. He would like another, but four is already a good size for a family. She wants another, he wants to wait, she wants the kids close together so they can play, he wants to wait. She wears him down. Then sitting on the bed, she holds him and kisses him. Suddenly the two writhing hirsute bodies of Italian descent are grunting and grappling in coitus for the opportunity

to complete the act first. A lovely thought.

"Yes, it would appear obvious."

James and Antonio round the corner with Patrick Cotlin and William Dorey behind them.

"Mark, buddy, finally got my flat screen there?"

"Yeah, it is your new flat screen, just a few adjustments thought. We decided a retro look, you know, more square like. And also to downgrade the visual clarity so it is dirtier, that way we can ween you off of it to something more advanced."

Antonio stood by his desk.

"Wow, that was actually fairly well thought out. Did you think of that just in case I was here and you had to say something?"

"Yeah. It actually took me all day. I was nervous before I came here, so I made up a list of comebacks. It is hard to keep up with the perspicacity of the Cotlin group."

"Wow, perspicacity. Big word. How about you use…uh," Antonio looks to William Dorey who has already seated himself at this desk. "Hey William. What is the word of the day?"

William looks down to a daily calendar on his desk and peers up at Antonio. "Pecuniary."

"Yeah, try using pecuniary in a sentence smart guy."

Mark plugs a cable into the back of the monitor, and turns it on. A blue light flutters as life is brought back into the machine.

"If the Cotlin group had a pecuniary measurement different than the U.S. dollar for the amount of their clients' wealth, for example the Mexican peso, they would seem like prodigies of the investment industry."

"Funny, funny," Antonio said with a smile acidly.

"The regal Mr. Sciarelli will find himself impecunious during the upbringing of his children."

Antonio gave a wry smile. "I don't have to wait, it is happening right now. I don't even dare use my credit cards, my wife has probably already maxed them out."

"You're the one who gave them to her," Sue piped up from the corner.

"Yeah, well, marriage is about compromise. And by compromise I mean bending completely to your wife's will."

"Yeah buddy, that is what I like to hear. You are already broken. She didn't need a few years, just a few kids," James chimes in sitting at his desk with his hands splayed behind his head.

"Who are you kidding, she had me as putty in her hand when we were sophomores in high school," Antonio confessed. "Mark, just do me a favor when you get married. When you say no, make sure that she understands it is no."

"Mark do me a favor. When you get married, don't remember any of Sciarelli's marriage advice," Ron shouted over.

"Please guys. Marriage? I am twenty four."

"I got married when I was twenty two," Antonio says.

"Yeah, and look how that turned out," James said.

"Nah. I don't need a wife. I think I would rather have a boat."

"You know, not a bad idea. Maybe I should call off the wedding," James rubs his chin in pensive thought.

"No, you need someone to take care of you. James, you are horrible alone," Antonio says.

"Thanks bud. Looking at you, I realize married life is the best choice."

Mark stepped out of Antonio's desk area.

"Thanks guys for all the advice. I have taken it to heart and will most assuredly think about it whenever I meet a woman. I have no doubt that it will help me in my future with the fairer gender and all of you have proven to be great sagacious men of the times," Mark said with an air of sarcasm. "Now, if you will excuse me, I have another computer to replace."

"Yeah Mark, you go do your work. Just wait until you meet your wife, then you will understand," Antonio said as Marked walked away.

Another monitor in his arms, Mark entered the office of a broker off of the main hallway. The broker was not a large producer, and did not speak very much to Mark. In fact it was a surprise to Mark when he called him and told him the monitor was broken, because Mark was unsure of who exactly it was.
Walking into the office, Mark put the monitor on the desk and looked around. The broker was out for the afternoon which meant Mark could take care of the minor problem at his leisure. He looked from wall to wall and saw a reprint of a Salvador Dali painting. Three African masks placed in a diagonal descent next to the painting. A banker's desk lamp that dated to sometime back in the twenties. Twelve baseball and pee wee football awards of the son of the broker placed on the opposite wall, and a coffee table next to the door that left just two inches to move the chair that was stuck in the room should any clients decide to come in.
After surveying the room, Mark said to himself, "Trust your instincts, your thoughts and your feelings; just don't trust your taste."

Stepping into the apartment, Mark feels a lack of energy and also needs to go to the bathroom at the same moment. Putting his bags down in his room he found his copy of Something Happened, by Joseph Heller. He trudged to the bathroom and closed the door and locked it. Turning on the light and fan, the low whirr of the fan masked any outside noise. Mark disrobed and sat on the toilet cracking open the book to the last page he had read. There was a radiator to his left, and it had just started another cycle. Mark read for twenty minutes without stopping to think. He looked around the small room, the warmth from the radiator, the lack of sounds of the outside. He finished with the toilet and stood up. About to put his clothes back on, he decided to do something. He pulled the bathroom rug closer to the radiator, and took his bath towel from the rack. Curling up next to the radiator, he read his book and felt the warmth creep in to his skin. There was no sound coming to bother or annoy him and he felt alone.

Chapter 19 - Finicky

Walking out of the elevator from lunch Ron Dunstmeyer pushed against the magnetic doors to get into the hallways. As he pushed the door open he heard a jiggle in the upper right. He noticed the air pump that opens and closes the door was slightly loose. He looked around the lobby and saw no one was watching. Taking out a paper clip from his pocket he broke off an end and stuffed it into an opening in the air tube. When the tube moved it now had the sound of a piece of metal rolling inside of it.
As he stepped through the door he almost knocked down Kenny.
Kenny was a frail old Irishman who had worked at the office for forty-five years. He started as a mail clerk, and over time the technology changed, but Kenny's position in the office didn't. Where there was a machine to be used, or a paper to be filed, that is what Kenny did. Now in his frail old age he manned the fax machines. His job was to send out faxes. Also he collected incoming faxes. When there was not a fax issue, he was talking to his wife, Sharon, on the phone. She called at least once every hour. She had a problem with the apartment, the cold, the wind, the sun, the refrigerator, the lights, the radio, milk, the kids outside, her sisters, and anything else at the moment. Kenny always offered advice, but it was rarely taken.

"Hey Ken," Mark said.
Craning his neck around and looking slightly to the side of Mark, Ken recognized him.
"Hello Mark. How's it going?" Kenny had lived in Boston since he was twenty-two, but still had a thick Irish accent.
"Not bad Ken. I am just fixing the fax machines so that it shows who sends the faxes."
"Oh, that's good."
Joanne had instructed Mark to program the feature so they could track the outgoing faxes better.
With the ever present fear of being sued, only brokers who had a fax machine were allowed to use their own machine. If someone without authorization used it, then the broker and the company is liable to be responsible for the outgoing piece(s) of information.
What brought this about was when a broker in a branch office in Omaha jokingly used another brokers machine, and when he sent a pornographic cartoon to another broker in the office. There were three problems that resulted from this 'joke.'
1 – The broker used another brokers machine without permission, thus whatever

he sent would be interpreted as originating from the broker who owned the machine.

2 – Every outgoing fax has a duplicate sent to the human resources department so they can review the faxes of their broker to make sure nothing is sent out against company policy, the New York Stock Exchange or the Securities and Exchange Commission is being sent out.

3 – The broker misdialed the number, and instead of going to another broker in the office it went to the local headquarters for NOW (National Organization of Women). The intern that manned the fax machine at the headquarter of the Omaha branch of NOW, took the copy to her section chief. The section chief sent a copy to the regional manager. The regional manager sent a copy to the executive headquarters. A PR rep for NOW contacted a Randley Financial Brokerage PR rep, and asked for an explanation.

The next day Kenny came around to Mark's desk. Sitting behind his computer, Mark saw Kenny's slow limping walk. His cane was in his right hand, and there was a slight swinging motion with his hip so he could bring his left leg around. As Kenny walked, Mark wanted dearly to run around his desk and pickup Kenny and bring him to where he wanted to go.

Kenny swings his head with his body, his mouth slightly agape. A glisten of saliva could be seen from the corner of his mouth as he heaved breaths in and out.

Mark could see Kenny in a street. Long tan trench coat going down to his ankles and wide black hat covering his white haired head. Walking down the street, he goes over a vent grate for the subway.

A train rushes by underground. A rush of wind comes underneath. Kenny looks down to see the bottom of his coat filling with air. It furls out rigidly in an umbrella like fashion. He looks momentarily like a southern belle going to a ball before a stronger gush of wind shoots him up like a rocket into the sky. All that is left is his cane stuck on the grate.

"Mark," Kenny says panting and sucking the saliva back in.

"Yeah Ken, what's up?"

"After you programmed the fax machines yesterday I found Erin using the Berger fax," Ken says in his this Irish accent in between breathes. His open weary mouth curves into a toothy grin.

"That's great Ken. Hopefully it will stop more people from using the wrong fax."

"Yeah." Ken pats the desk with his left hand and limps away to the break room to make some coffee.

Chapter 20 - Fat Head

Sitting at his desk, Mark had his finger in between the buttons of his shirt. He was trying to secretively work out the lint in his belly button. While doing this he was multitasking, by thinking about how different life would be if he had an outtie.

The phone line for Matilda lit up on Mark's phone. She was not in her office, so he picked up the line.

"Randley Financial Brokerage Financial Services, how may I help you?"

"Hello, I want to speak to the manager."

The voice was that of an elderly lady and was very gruff. From the tone the lady was using, it was obvious she was upset.

"Um, I am sorry, but the manager is not in right now," Mark lied. Running interference for his bosses was part of the job. "Can I help you with something."

"No, not unless you can give me my money back. I have had bad service with you people, and I want my money back with interest." Mark had a vague feeling that he was in a McDonalds.

"Um, well, let's see what we can do. What seems to be the problem?"

"Well sonny boy, the problem is that you people have been tossing me around like a piece of meat, and I want it to stop. I don't want to be bullied or pushed into some investment and I want to get the money back that I lost."

"Well, first let's start with your account. What is your account number?"

There was a ruffling of papers at the other end of the line. "I am looking for it. Just you wait to see."

"If you don't know your account number the social security number will be fine."

After telling him her social security number the account for an Alice Shaw came up.

"Ms. Shaw?"

"That's right."

"Alright, well let's see what your account says. You are currently a house account, which means that you are part of the branch here, but not under a specific broker right now."

"Well I have been passed around through three brokers. They all should be in there."

"Actually our system doesn't show a past history of the brokers on the account, just the current broker on the account."

"I bet that fat head went in and erased himself so he they wouldn't know it was him."

"Pardon ma'am?"

"That stupid Ted Harris, or whatever his name was. He bullied me into investing in bond and I want my money back."

"We have a Ned Harris here, is that who you are talking about?"

"Yeah, that's him. Fat 'Head Harris.' You know what happened with him? I will tell you what happened." Mark felt the sudden urge to put the phone down and get a cup of coffee, but decided to listen.

"I was sent over to that fat head because I don't have a million dollars. That is what you people do, when you don't have enough money you just send someone to where you can manipulate them. You people tried that with me, but it didn't work cause' I am too smart," she cleared her throat. "I called up that Ned who was my broker and asked him if he would buy a triple B rated bond. A triple B, that is a good rating, don't you think?"

"For some bonds that is a very good rating ma'am."

"Well, I wanted to buy that bond, and he wouldn't buy it for me. That stupid fat head Ned. He then just bullied me into buying a triple A rated bond, and I want my money back, and into the triple B and also want to be compensated for the money I lost on the bond."

"Well, that may have been Ned's thought on the matter. Triple A is a higher rating than triple B."

"I want the triple B. I want my money, and you and your flunky idiot friend Ned aren't going to swindle me again."

"Ma'am, I don't think that Ned was trying to swindle you, but we will see what we can do. I am going to have my manager call you back and explain what options there are to you."

"Manager, the manager of the office?"

"No, I will have the administration manager Matilda Hew call you back and she will explain what options there are to you."

"I don't want no stupid administration manager. I want the manager of the office right now."

"As I explained ma'am, he is not in the office right now. My admin manager will get back to you shortly though."

"Shortly, what does that mean? Does that mean in an hour, in three hours, in a day?"

"No ma'am. She will get back to you as soon as she gets back to her office."

"Oh, so she is out too. Is anybody there? Does anybody work there? Do you people care about your clients at all?"

"Yes ma'am, we care very much for our clients' interests. Now I will explain the problem to my admin manager and she will get back to you shortly."

"No, I want to speak to the manager of the office and I am not hanging up until I get that stupid fat head."

Mark suddenly realized the power she had. He could not just hang up on her, phone calls were occasionally recorded, and even if they weren't she was a client and hanging up on a client would be wrong.

"As I explained before ma'am the manager is out of his office. I can have the admin manager call you back very shortly."

"Look, I have a complaint and I want the manager to listen to my complaint and give me my money back."

Mark thought to himself about the impossibility of giving money back to a client. If firms did that, then there wouldn't be any investment banks because they would all be broke.

"The manager is not in his office today, and it is the admin manager that would take care of the problem in this type of situation."

"Can this Matilda give me my money back?"

"Matilda can guide you towards a solution to your problem Miss Shaw."

"She will just push me off to another flunky is what she will do. I don't want to talk to Matilda, I want to talk to the manager."

"He is not in his office right now, and Matilda is the one who would take care of the problem."

"Look, I am not hanging up until I speak to your manager, so you just better transfer me to him and let me tell him I want my money."

Mark realized his head was sunk low and his arms were trying to keep his head up as he pleaded with this senile woman.

"Ma'am, he is not in the office right now. Matilda Hew the admin manager is the one who would listen to the problem and guide you towards a solution. I will have Matilda call you back very shortly, and she will speak to you."

"I don't want to talk to any Matilda. She is just another of your flunkies, and will just try to pass me off because I am not a millionaire. I have some money, I am not nothing. Do you think I am nothing?"

Mark so desperately wanted to say yes. Wanted to scream yes, wanted to let out all of the air in his lungs so this woman could understand the amount of stress and disgust she was creating in Mark.

"No ma'am, I do not think that. But I can have my admin manager get back to you very shortly."

"I don't want to talk to the admin manager; I want to talk to the manager."

Twenty minutes later.

"Ma'am, the manager is not in the office right now. I will have the admin manager call you back at the earliest convenience."

"Convenience, whose convenience? Not mine. I want my money back. I don't want to be bullied by fat heads or jerks."

"Ma'am I will have the admin manager call you back very shortly. She will be

able to handle the situation with you."
Mark felt weary. He wanted to end the conversation.
A moment of epiphany happened.
"I don't want any admin manager; I want to speak to the head of the office."
"Ms. Shaw, I apologize, but I have to take care of something right now. I have your phone number and the pertinent information and I will have my admin manager call you back as soon as possible. Thank you Ms. Shaw." Mark hung up the phone as soon as the word Shaw was out of his mouth.
He was free. He was free.
Matilda came back ten minutes later from lunch, and Mark explained the story.
"This is going to be a fun conversation. Thanks so much, in the future, there is a phone number for customer complaints."
"Yeah, cool, have fun."
Mark sat in his chair and saw that Matilda picked up her line. She got through to Alice Shaw and explained her courses of action, which was calling the number for customer complaints. Matilda was polite, accommodating, and after five minutes of listening to the woman, she told her that she had to go take care of paperwork and abruptly hung up.
Walking into her office, Mark saw an expression of surprise on Matilda's face.
"That is one crazy lady."

Around two thirty in the afternoon Mark had a call come from Nancy at the switchboard for the office.
"Hey Nance, what's up."
"I, uh, have a lady that wants to talk to the manager, but she doesn't know his name. I don't think that this is a person who should talk to Richard, so is it OK if I transfer her to you?"
"Let me guess, Alice Shaw."
"Oh, you know her?"
"Yeah, we've met."
"OK, here you go."
Mark waited for a few seconds. He wanted to stall for as long as he could.
"Hello, Randley Financial Brokerage Financial Services."
"I want to speak to the manager."
"I am sorry, he is not in his office right now, can I take a message and have him call you back?"
"No, you can't take a message, I want to talk to that fat head."
"Unfortunately he is not here right now, but I can have him call you back."
"Look, I want to talk to the manager. My money is in there with you people, and I can talk to the manager if I want to."
"Um, ma'am, he is not in the office right now. I can take a message if you like

and have him or someone else call you back."

"Someone else, yeah that is it. You people are just fat heads. You all just pass me off to your flunkies and you don't even care about your clients."

"Ma'am we care very much for our clients. May I take your name and number so that I can let him know who called?"

"You don't know who this is?"

"Is this Ms. Shaw?"

"Yes it is. Don't just pass me off to some flunky like the last lady did. You said she was going to help me get my money back, and all she did was send me somewhere to tell them I think you guy manipulated and bullied me. That is what you all are, just bullies."

"Ma'am, I am sure that the employees here are not that rude. Now I have your name and number, and I will have my admin manager get back to you as soon as possible."

"I want the manager to call me back. That Matilda lady is just tacky, and I don't want her to push me off again. I want to give that manager a piece of what his clients think of him, and I don't want to be pushed off to some flunky."

"Ma'am, I can have my admin manager call you back very shortly, and she will be able to tell you if there is anything else you can do besides the customer service number. Do you still have that number ma'am?"

"Yes I still have that number, but I don't want to speak to them. They are all flunkies, and you are too."

"Well ma'am, I know that I am not. But thank you for calling, and I will give my manager the message." Mark let the phone down on the receiver and felt sad about old age.

The next morning Mark walked into work, and saw Matilda sitting behind her desk laughing loudly.

"Mark, come in here. You will never believe it."

Mark walked into the office.

"That Alice Shaw woman left four messages on my voicemail last night. She actually filled up all the space in four voicemail messages. She has been calling me tacky, the office fat heads and does not like Richard at all. Do me a favor, when I get old, shoot me."

Matilda cackled and shut the voicemail off.

Chapter 21 - Transition

Mark woke up a half hour early. It is Tuesday, May second. For two and a half months Mark has been ticking off the days until this one. It is a month before he will leave Randley Financial Brokerage. Matilda has been nice to him, so he doesn't want to give only a two week notice knowing how difficult it will be to find someone stupid enough to take the job.
Mark gets out of bed since he can't sleep and makes waffles. He tops them with fruit, cream and honey.
Feeling warm and refreshed he saunters into the bathroom to take a shower. Putting on his suit, he made his tie especially straight, and walks out of the apartment.
With plenty of time to make the morning metro, he enjoyed the Boston spring morning, and kicked the leaves in the street.
Getting into the office, he walked to his desk and put his bag down.
"Hey Miss."
"Hey Mark."
Matilda had her nose in a file, and didn't seem too intent on moving.

11:17 a.m.
That is the time Mark had decided to walk into Matilda's office and tell her that he is quitting. He wasn't sure if he should be quiet and respectful; loud, boisterous and playful; or even possibly strip off his suit and start a fire at the entrance of her office while chanting something incomprehensible while throwing his excrement willy nilly in the air.
Mark judged that it was a pleasant time, since Matilda would still be in a partial drugged state from her morning caffeine doses, and it will be just before lunch. The conversation would probably run a half hour and afterwards she would want to go to lunch and gossip with Joanne about it.
Mark sat down at his desk. After entering his password he smiled and said in a low tone, "I'm fucking out of here."

Staring at the clock in the lower right of his computer monitor, it turned to 11:17. Matilda was on the phone. It was alright, it could wait a few moments.
11:22 a.m.
Matilda puts her phone down. Now is the time.
Mark stands up. He walks the ten feet to Matilda's office slowly. She looks up from a file as he enters the office.
"Hey Miss, got a second?"
"Yeah, sure, what's up?"

Mark enters the room and closes the door. He knows that by closing the door he is in effect silently telling Matilda that it is important, and not for anyone else. Mark sits leisurely in the chair facing Matilda's desk.

"Well," Mark takes a breath, and lets it out.

"This place fucking sucks. I come in to work daily and wonder about my existence. I know that I am not smart, but a monkey could do my job. I personally don't understand why the people here aren't put away for being absolutely devoid of feeling and natural common sense. It seems that since I have taken this job not only have I had the problem of feeling like an inept pigeon fluttering around retarded park, but I go home and have little energy to actually find a life that feels like something closer to contentment. Working for you has been difficult, but you are not really the problem that I have with this place because you are just doing what you have to so you can have a home for your family. It is the whole fucking stupid system here that is bent on being as organized and productive as possible, except that it fails to add any semblance of creativity or freedom. In working here I have wanted to destroy the office, but to what conclusion? No amount of explosive force would be able to destroy the apathy that this place creates. I could liquidate everyone here and in two weeks the place would be reconstructed, and reemployed with new people just as mindless and afraid as before. I think that, in fact, that is the reason that this place exists. The fear. The absolute, irresolute fear that runs through every worker bee in the place. The people in this office come in here so that they can make money, be part of money, and in the end try to be rich. Very few are rich, very few actually make it to that point, but this place drives that sensation in the heart of the people here. That stupid dream that you can actually have unfathomable amounts of money and be something untouchable.

I don't want to be sad anymore. I don't want to go home and feel depressed at having just wasted eight hours of my life doing something inane and without any real reason. I would like to live my short life feeling like I actually do something that I like and feel happy about it. If I can't feel happy, at least I would like to feel content."

Mark stands up now. "I am fucking done with this place. I am done with this stupid shit and I don't want any more people trying to tell me that this is a good opportunity or a good experience. This whole place has little reason except to be a reminder of what not to do, and what not to be in this world."

"Well, yeah, I do have something important to talk about."

Matilda closes the file and looks curiously at Mark as he sits down in the chair. "I have been thinking about this for a little while, and I think that it is time for me to leave."

Matilda's face goes from an expression of curiosity to shock.

"I think that I want to start traveling again, and my time in Boston has been fun, but I think that I would like to try something new and see some new things."

"Wow, this is surprising. I mean, good for you, really. Wow. Well, I guess that it was going to happen at some point, but, well, just wow."

"Yeah, I know, it is kind of sudden, but it is something that I have been thinking about for a little while, and I think that it would be best. I mean, I am just a kid, and I should go and be a kid for a while."

"Yeah, you're right."

"I am giving a month notice though. I am not going to leave you in a lurch with just two weeks. I would like to leave at the end of the month if that is alright."

"Thank god, yes, yes please. I hope we can find somebody in that time."

"Hopefully, but I know it might be a little difficult."

"Well, we will find somebody." Matilda looked into her hands. "So, wow, that is cool. You are going to go travel? Where are you going to go?"

"I think I am going to go back to California and see some friends that I haven't seen since college, and then go on into Mexico and the Caribbean. I have saved my money since I got here, so I think I should be able to travel for around five or six months. Really I would like to go for as long as possible, but we will see how long that will be."

"Wow, that sounds like a great trip. It really sounds awesome."

Chapter 22 - Depart

Descending the elevator, Mark felt lighter. It might have been just that the elevator was going down, but it also might have been that he would never have to go back up.

Walking out of the lobby Mark felt anonymous, as if somehow there was nothing left of him in that building. He was just another body that passed through the doors.

Walking out of the building he didn't turn back. He could feel the building at his back, but it didn't matter, he kept walking.

Made in United States
Orlando, FL
20 June 2024